THE STRANDS

Brian White

Dark Revelations Media LLC

Warning: This book is intended for mature audiences.

ISBN 978-1-944830-01-4

Published by Dark Revelations Media LLC. For more information about authors and upcoming books visit:

www.darkrevmedia.com

Masks of God – The Tin Man

A childhood prank turns violent, giving Austin his first glimpse of true evil. Traumatized, branded a coward, this Tin Man goes in search of his heart, embarking on a mysterious journey that brings him in contact with shamans, monks, occultists, and otherworldly beings that tell of a Mask that can unlock hidden powers of those who wear it. Will the Mask reveal the secret Tin has been searching for? Or will his obsession with it lead only to insanity? Only the Mask can tell.

Get you FREE ebook copy at: https://darkrevmedia.com/mogt-inman

CHAPTER 1

There is a thought that drives man insane;
A system of logic that attempts to make sense of the senseless;
And there is a strand that binds them, making sense of the insane.

Jonathan Romero threw his head back, the three Tylenol capsules sliding to the back of his throat. He gazed out his office window as he brought the tumbler of whisky to his lips to wash the pills down. It was early for a drink but he didn't care. The combination was meant to ease the pounding in the back of his skull that resulted from the frustrations of the past week. The project meeting he'd returned from was simply another example of corporate banality topped by drudgery, making the dark cancerous secret in his brain pulse with black malignancy.

He took another sip, the pleasant burn delectably scorching his throat. The whisky's smoky aroma brought out his contemplative side as he surveyed Philadelphia's historic buildings reflected in the mirrored faces of the skyscrapers that surrounded his office. At the center was the promise and hope of the American rebels that had signed the Declaration of Independence, the hall where the first continental congress had met, where the altruistic citizens had listened to the first ringing of the Liberty Bell. At its edges were the gleaming towers of commercialism that had risen in the wake of revolution, selling the promise of the American Dream in shrink-wrapped packages for the sheep who could afford to purchase it.

He caught the ghost of his reflection in the window, his vision clouding, the scene changing to an unformed amalgam of images waiting to be formed by the creative instinct of some grand architect. "The strands of life spin and evolve within the infinite carpet of the Self," he whispered into his glass, taking another swallow. He felt the first hint of the warm comfort beginning to deaden the atonal requiem in his skull, caused by the tumor hiding within its depths. The ugly gray growth in his temporal lobe represented the reaper that pursued him, chasing him with scythe raised, and harvest time was coming soon—too soon.

But not yet. For now, the dull throb deep in his cerebral cortex compelled him to examine all he could, question all he could, learn all he could, before it was too late, before it was all over.

There was a knock at the door. He blinked and the city returned to its previous state, bricks and mortar coalescing back to their rightful place, the citadels of industry once again reflecting broken promises, forgotten ideals and lost hope. He sighed and rubbed his temples. "Come in."

The door flung open and Macaria walked briskly into his office. He brightened temporarily as he saw her. She wasn't given to cheerful emotions, but he saw the hint of a smile at the corner of her lips, which in turn made him smile. Then the corners of her mouth turned down as she spotted the glass in his hand. Stupid, he told himself. I shouldn't have let her see me drinking at work. He put the tumbler down on his desk next to the List. The pounding in his skull sent a spasm through his brain, but he pushed back, fighting it.

"I forgot we had a meeting scheduled," he said by way of apology.

Her eyes darkened with concern. Her dilated pupils examined him as if he were one of her targets, searching for a weak point—not to kill, not to exploit, but to assess whether he was all right. That cold and clinical stare sent a shiver down the fault line of his spine, and under her continued scrutiny the initial shiver became a full-on nervous system quake that vibrated through his body.

"I see," was her only reply, but he could read the subtext in her tone and her body language as she avoided looking at the whisky glass. What she saw, with those keen perceptive eyes, is that he would have put the glass and bottle away if he'd remembered they had an appointment. He would have hidden what he was doing, not changed it.

"I have little to report," Macaria said. "No updates on the activities of the Conductors. There is one fully dedicated to your research and project, but he's not uncovered anything yet."

Romero grunted. He'd not raised his hopes too high that the Conductors could find a cure for his cancer in the Strands, but whenever he heard another negative report he couldn't help but give some dissatisfied reply.

"The other four are currently working on various other projects that are in their infant phases: a weapon that works by canceling out vibrational frequencies, a communication technology that maps sound waves to brain patterns, and one that I found intriguing, a tone generator that can manipulate emotions using various music scales and chords." Despite her claim, nothing in her tone indicated any interest at all. This quick status update was delivered like standard corporate chatter, with no obvious sentiment. Is there anything that gives her pleasure? One thing. He cringed at the thought and waved his hand, prompting her to continue.

"These projects are still in the early phases so we are still assessing whether or not patents need to be pursued. Nothing filed with the patent office in the past two weeks." Another brief pause to give him a moment to interject if needed; this time she does not need to be prompted to continue.

"The Watcher has reported that he may have observed Alex reaching out to someone through a dream, but he can't be sure. He caught only a glimpse."

"Blake William?"

She placed her report on his desk next to the List. Her gaze lingered there for a moment before returning to Romero. "Yes."

No surprise. No questioning how he knew that. But he felt compelled to explain his seemingly prophetic response.

"William became known to the Board because of his books on mysticism and the occult. He fit the profile of someone Alex might reach out to. To Alex he would be the perfect recruit because his poetry and writing could in turn influence others. Also, their psyche profiles are very similar. They are made for each other, Alex with his theories on mystical physics feeding William's poetry and occult philosophy. They'd drive each other to madness."

"You miss Alex"

It wasn't a question, but Romero took it as such. Did he? Could he be honest even with himself when it came to Alex and their relationship? What it had meant—still meant... he shook it off. "Even if I did, that wouldn't change anything. William has been placed on the List. That is what matters right now. My feelings towards Alex are irrelevant."

Macaria's eyes brightened, the corners of her lips rising ever so slightly. And there was the look Romero dreaded seeing on her features, the one that only arose when they spoke of death or the List. Pleasure and something even deeper—ecstasy? As soon as the topic of assassination was on the table, she began to salivate like a starving tiger that just had meat thrown into its cage.

"I want you only to observe for the moment. I want to see if we can use William to find Alex somehow. Keep the Watcher focused on William; maybe Alex will try to contact him again. In the mean time you can physically follow William in case Alex tries to contact him by more direct means."

The emotionless stare was back, the steak temporarily removed from her plate.

That black stare, clinical and calculating, brought forth a paradox of thoughts for Romero. For him the extinction of the Shadows was both a relief and regret. There was relief that he would not have to raise more children to embrace murder and violence as a way of life and regret that such a lineage would end. Strand Corp. was doing away with tradition as quickly as it could, turning away from founding principles to become a monster of industry. The Board, with its myopic wisdom, had decided that the Shadows and the art of assassination were remnants of a bygone era and no longer needed to be maintained. Macaria, the culmination of centuries of breeding and training would be the last and with her death would go the last vestiges of the ancient code of the Strand Society. Contemplating the actions of such a powerful and morally bankrupt corporation made Romero shiver.

But the world was moving on from tradition. The fact that Macaria was the first woman Shadow may have been harbinger to that end. Kevin and Alisha Tully, descendants of the legendary Jonathan Tully, had been capable of having only one child. They had tried unsuccessfully to conceive again, and when the doctor had finally informed them that having another child would be impossible, Macaria became the last Shadow. Romero remembered the first time he had seen Macaria. Kevin and Alisha were each holding one of her hands. He read the pain in their faces and wondered how hard it must be to complete this part of their oath. How heartbreaking. Romero wondered if he could perform his duty and take her from them. Innocent brown eyes stared up at him; she pulled away from her parents and extended a soft delicate hand to him. So soft, so beautiful, could he turn such a thing into a machine of death? Without a word spoken the transaction was completed, the final Tully oath fulfilled and Romero's soul damned. All that pain and hardship meant something in the context of tradition and purpose but the Board had transformed it all to worthlessness. Now the Tully's pain, his, Macaria's meant next to nothing.

Romero was also the last. The last to give a shit. The last who cared or even remembered the credo of the original Strand Society: "To protect the miracles of the Strands and to enhance and support the spiritual evolution of humanity." The tumor pulsed. Who was he kidding? Even he was more concerned with himself than humanity. The Strands were a tool to the Board, and a tool to him. He'd traded his search for miracles for questing after world power and selfishness. He was now more tool than soul.

The silence had become uncomfortable, his ruminating deadening the air between them. He wanted to say something fatherly, something loving.

"Your father and mother would be proud of you for fulfilling the oath the way you have."

She looked at him askance, trying to determine the remark's source. It fit neither the present conversation nor Romero's normal callous, businesslike demeanor.

"You are the only family I have ever known." She turned from his gaze. "Are you proud of me?"

He took a moment to try and frame exactly how he felt. Loving her like a daughter didn't necessarily mean he approved of her actions. She was a gleaming sword that inspired respect but also fear. No matter how he dressed it up, no matter how ornamental he made the hilt, in the end he couldn't change its nature. She was designed to bring death. He couldn't bring himself to accept it.

"I'm in awe of your talents and abilities," he hedged.

"That is not what I asked."

It was Romero's turn to look away. He picked up the tumbler again, swirled the ochre liquid in the glass, and took another sip, avoiding the fire shooting out of her eyes. "I know. I'm not sure how to answer that question."

He pictured her taking out a gun, training it on his forehead, and pulling the trigger, splashing his brains on the office window, a bloody epitaph. He knew what she was capable of. But she only carried out his orders. In that respect he was responsible for the dark being she had become.

"You have done everything I ever asked. If there is any shame in it, it is mine," he finally said.

"That is only another deflection. Would you be proud if I were an artist, a surgeon? Would you be proud if I were the best at what I did regardless of what that was?"

He rubbed his temples. "My head hurts, I'm sorry. I'm not thinking straight right now."

"I would think a reminder of how close death is would bring out your more paternal instincts."

She turned away, clearly aggravated with him. Why? Because I'm drinking before noon? Because I wasn't a good father? I was never meant to be a father. Then just say that. Just tell her. She is the only family you will ever have. But he was too used to living with secrets, living the lie.

"Too true," was all he said, sighing.

Recovering his persona of the director of one of the largest corporations on the planet, he added, "Do not bring my condition up again while in this building. If the Board were to know their response could be catastrophic for both of us."

"Of course."

Without another word she picked up her report from the desk and left the office, closing the door silently behind her as if to prove to him that she had control of her anger and was not going to let his responses affect her.

Romero sat and threw back the last of the whisky. Staring across his desk, he picked out the name Blake William. Number two on the List, only surpassed by Alex Tannersly, who had been number one for some time. Going from Board member to rogue agent gave him the exalted status of terrorist.

"Blake William." He spoke the name reverentially. This one felt different, felt dangerous. The rest of the List was filled with people whom the Board couldn't discredit, or who had become a danger to them financially or legally. But William had no financial motives, no disputes over intellectual property that had been pilfered from his dreams or thoughts. He was a man who was comfortable staring into the abyss to see what it offered, seeking a dragon's lair and hoping to find treasure there. And here was Romero, the dragon, protecting trinkets and gems that had long since ceased to sparkle or offer him any promise. He no longer knew why he was protecting them. It was just instinct. Hide it, protect it, kill it. The new credo of Strand Corporation.

The List grew shorter every year, filling Romero with contradictory emotions. For it meant that few came in search of the dragon's lair anymore, the world preferring the glossy, neon-glaring constructed reality of commercialism, materialism, and passive consumerisms to the divine light of art, poetry and mysticism. As Thomas Agrippa had stated at the last Board meeting in his characteristically sarcastic tone "You're a dinosaur, Romero, a relic, as are the Shadows. Strand Corporation is a business and will be run as such. Your contributions were appreciated but are becoming unnecessary and will be sunset upon your retirement." This was the typical type of response Romero received whenever he inquired about new Shadow recruits.

Macaria's devotion to Romero was the only thing stopping the Board from putting him on the List, and he knew it. They feared her because they no longer lived in a world governed by violence and killing, and had no idea how to deal with people of that world. If they were to decide he was going to be "retired" early, they would take her first—if they could.

He looked past the List to the window. The Persian carpet on the floor of his office cast its spectral reflection onto the glass, hovering over the city. His perception shifted and he saw the filaments separating, spreading, and becoming the threads that created the carpet of the city, Independence Hall, Met Life, the cars, the people, all the individual strands that made up a small part of the fabric of reality. Each strand was thousands of threads, each thread millions of molecules, each molecule made of atoms, subatomic particles, on and on. The complexity compounded the deeper one went. Mystics went in search of that one strand that would identify the pattern, that one strand that would explain it all. It was this image, this comparison, that had given rise to the name of the conceptual framework of the universe. It was why when Jonathan Tully, George Mason, and others had come to America in search of religious and ideological tolerance, they had named their small group the Strand Society. It was a society that had existed for centuries in various forms knowing that it must transform and incorporate the ideals of each age in order to be effective. That belief in progress through change could ironically bring about its end.

"Christ," Romero muttered under his breath, blinking as his vision returned to normal. The dull world came back into focus, replacing the glory of the miraculous. Its glimmering surfaces only hid the rot and decay that were slowly eating at it from the inside. And once the heart was dead, the façade would fall away and all that would be left was ash. The Strand Society had hoped to prevent that condition, when it fled Europe with its revolutionary ideas, and brought them to the philosophically fertile soil of America. But the roots of those ideals had been twisted into the credos and charters of Strand Corporation which strove to create and nurture this slow death.

The ethereal fingers of his tumor spread into his brain, releasing thoughts from dark subterranean parts of his mind that he rarely explored. Reaching down into the gloomy haze, they dug into the deeper tunnels of his cortex to trigger a memory of a concept he read about long ago in a book on comparative mythology, a theory that stated that all stories were one. That like the weave, they might contain seemingly different characters on different stages with different tasks and novel actions, but in the end there was only one story to be told, and that one story was as much a part of humankind as our genes or our blood.

Sages, saviors, seers, and sorcerers had searched the ancient places for this one tale. Fearlessly they went in search of that one strand that would tell the whole story, that would explain the truth. And once it was found, they realized that the truth had been in front of them all along. The story of the shaman, the medieval knight, the buccaneer, and the Jedi was humanity's story—the story of the human quest for meaning. It was this one story that was both the alpha and the omega. It was this archetypal story that took the questing characters from beginning to end only to reveal a new beginning.

Would Romero's slow death, and all it represented, mean nothing in the end? Was that the Reaper's curse, to reveal that his life was only another iteration of a story that spun on forever, heedless of anyone's efforts to understand or halt it?

Romero closed his eyes. The city made of intertwined threads glittered in his inner vision.

He hoped it wasn't true.

He hoped it was.

CHAPTER 2

In a tiny, cluttered room, Blake William tossed and turned, and dreamed of being William Blake.

The wind blew through the tall grasses surrounding him, adding its soft voice to that of the stream that babbled to his left. The two sounds combined into a unified voice that spoke the story of all life. He breathed deeply, momentarily content with the All, wishing he could hold on to that moment and expand it eternally so that the fear would never return. But the feeling was as fleeting as the wind, and the more he struggled to hold on to it, the faster it seemed to disappear.

Heaven was here somewhere. He searched for it in the brook, the grass, the hills, the dandelion seeds that danced in the embrace of the wind. With pen in hand, he tried to capture its beauty, hoping to reveal some deeper light that penetrated and moved throughout all life, but thus far he'd revealed only shadow: ink staining the purity of the white page, thoughts marring the perfection of Being.

The veil of illusion he'd peeled back had been protecting his sanity, and now he saw the world raw and dark, a gloomy, forbidding landscape that was home to demons that poisoned the mind. It was their venomous bite with its power to bring on insanity that he feared.

He closed his eyes, praying for deliverance. The air grew colder around him, pleasant humidity giving way to dampness and the stench of rot, and he knew there would be no deliverance today. "Not again," he begged as a shudder ran up his spine, shaking him to his icy core.

"Hello?" A mere whisper. A sound that could easily be mistaken for wind, grass, or brook and then summarily forgotten. William wished he could fool himself like that. Most men could. They could turn away, swear off drinking, and return to their predictable lives where the dead didn't walk or speak. But William Blake had learned that he was not a man. He was something more, something else; something... other.

"Are you the Blake?" The question held a hint of reverence, as if asking him whether he were the Christ. But the voice was also stronger. More Here than There. He thought the speaker was female but the voice was not yet Here enough for him to tell. In all his encounters with the dead he'd never been able to determine which party was crossing the ethereal line between life and death. Was he stepping into her territory or she into his. Would a spy on the far shore of the brook see her as a living person or would they watch in horror as William slowly became transparent and crossed into the gray limbo of the dead.

"I am," he whispered over his shoulder. Not turning. Not yet. The dead so rarely looked appealing to the living. Seeing past forms was a trick he had yet to master. Until he did there was his sanity to protect. If she did not beg his sight he would not offer it.

"William. If it pleases you?"

"William, then." Definitely more coherent, definitely a young woman's voice. It was tainted with sorrow and regret; perhaps she had died without having had the opportunity to taste much of what life had to offer.

"Names are such a useless convention. I learned that in death." She chuckled. "Or should I say more aptly, on this side of life. Do you want my name, William?"

He shook his head. "As you said—useless."

"I thought not. It must be so difficult for you, seeing both sides, knowing that there is no more hope in death than that offered in life. Makes it all seem so pointless when you think about it. And believe me, in death there is a lot of time to think. That's part of the irony of the whole thing, you know. Having all the time in the world and yet wanting nothing to do with it. Wishing every moment that time would just end so that you could be released. Don't you think that ironic?" She didn't pause for a response, simply sighed and continued. "But you. You are a prophet without a voice. You can tell no one directly, what you see, because then people would think you insane, making matters that much worse. It's almost—"

He didn't want to hear any more. He'd heard the philosophy of the dead and it was more depressing than that of the uninspired living. He cut her off.

"Your purpose, miss?" He knew he sounded dismissive, but he was aggravated.

"Miss, is it?" She sounded offended, mocking his tone.

"I'll call you dead thing if you wish. Dear, sweetheart, whatever you want, as long as you state your business with me. The dead draw too long a line to my door and as you were so astute in observing, I am alive and for me time is not something to waste." The last cut her. He could hear the hurt in the sharp shocked groan that followed. He didn't care. The business of the dead moved too slowly for one still alive.

There was vehemence in her tone. He could imagine her biting her tongue, wanting to spit back an insult. "I heard you have a temper. Biting wit or sarcasm depending on which side of the insult you are on. So odd in one who has the power to speak with the dead. But I guess—"

He began to rise and her last words caught fearfully in her throat, a whimper of surprise punctuating her sentence.

"I have all the knowledge I can deal with at the moment. Good day."

He began to walk away, conscious that her eyes were burning into his back, sorrow and anger fighting for dominance. The dead could be obstinate, believing for some reason that the living owed them something. In this case he hoped it was not death that she felt he was owed.

"Please." A throat-choking whisper on the edge of tears; sorrow taking prevalence.

"What then?"

"I died a young woman. I've had more experience on this side of life than on yours, but fear holds me here, a prisoner to what I value. Illusions concern me; demons of my own creation threaten to consume me."

He sat back down, feeling sorry for her. He felt a cold touch on his shoulder, attempting reconciliation. With her lips so close to his ear he could feel her frozen breath as she continued.

"In all of life I wished only to feel love. I died on a Tuesday thinking that true love would come to me on Wednesday. In every cloud I saw the promise of a tomorrow sun, a tomorrow love. It was always just another heartbeat away, until my heart stopped beating."

She paused and he could hear the indecision in her silence. She questioned the point of any of this. Was anything real or true? She must have decided because she continued.

"Then I heard the dead whisper of the Blake, the one who sees beyond the grave. I felt hope, wondering if maybe he—you—could help. Certainly one who sees beyond death must know something of love."

"I have shown you all the love I possess. You are searching for the wrong type of love. I don't know what—"

"A kiss."

"A kiss?"

"Yes. Just one kiss, a kiss that would make me believe, even if for only a moment, that love is possible."

He turned slowly. She was sitting close. His eyes drank her in. She was beautiful in a way that stopped his breath: black hair, brown eyes speckled with almond that sparkled gold in the reflected rays of the sun, full lips. Without verbalizing his answer he leaned in towards her. Her mouth opened slightly and instead of the rot of the grave he could smell the faint hint of citrus and peppermint. Her lips were even softer than he'd imagined, silkier. He seemed to melt into them, the heat of his passion emanating through every part of him. Leaning in further he felt as if he'd fallen into her; an abyss of passion. A light sparked in his brain and a warm flood of desire washed over him. For the first time in his life he knew what it was to be possessed by desire. He would give all to keep this feeling. All to possess such love.

Suddenly everything changed. There was a cold stabbing pain above the bridge of his nose. He pulled away from her and pressed his index finger to the spot, but there was nothing there, no blade, no hole, no blood. The phantom icy dagger pushed deeper, compressing reality to the tip of the blade. Somewhere far away a bell tolled. There was a fluttering, the sound of a thousand birds taking flight instantaneously, the buzz of flies. The ethereal knife was pulled back with a pop as the pressure was released.

He opened his eyes to see a man retreating slowly from him. The man dragged his left leg slightly as he walked a few paces before stopping and turning to stare back at him. Everything seemed sharp. The hum of the bees was symphonic, the grass bled green, dandelion seeds danced in the wind to the sound of a hummingbird's thunderously flapping wings. Time seemed to compress, the world slowing down, allowing him to observe the dust rising from the grass as the wind blew, the sun heliographing over the surface of the brook, scattered rays caught and expanded in the bird's feathers. Each sound echoed and reverberated as if the world were a concert hall capturing the music of life and replaying it back within the confines of this singular moment. And in the center of it all, out of place yet central to the scene, was the older man, leaning slightly to his right, observing him through light blue eyes. The man squinted slightly, adopting a shooter's stare, gauging all that surrounded him and calculating its effect on his one perfect shot.

"However much you think you see, Blake William, there is more."

Blake William, not William Blake. He was addressing the dreamer, not the dreamed.

The man began to move, his right hand and fingers twirling within the larger orbit of his circling arm. Blake felt pulled into the gravity of this hypnotic motion, his vision focusing on the display as pinpricks of color began to emerge from the dancing fingers. These dots of color merged to form strings, then bands, and finally a rainbow-rimmed ring. The dark center fluttered open, a dreamer's lids opening from sleep. Within this eye he saw an alien sky, a dark tower, a desert dwelling, the colors dancing before him, unleashing visions of other worlds and other lives. There was another whooshing sound as air from this alien landscape was sucked through the portal into his ordinary world. It carried with it the aroma of hermetic knowledge: musty, aged papyrus and leather from secret tomes hidden from the eyes of normal men. Beyond that was the sour smell of the fruit of the knowledge of good and evil, and the sweet heady nectar from the tree of immortal life. Underneath it was an alien scent he could not find words to describe. It promised new revelations, a way of seeing the world that was so new one could not comprehend it and then ever look at the world the same way again.

Blake ached to launch himself into the portal. He began to rise from the rock.

The portal winked closed mockingly, as if saying, "You can look but not touch."

For a moment he was angry.

The man spoke again. "Not yet. But soon."

Blake didn't understand. He didn't want to wait. He'd been waiting his whole life for something like this. Now he realized that in all the things he'd seen and experienced, this was what he was meant to find. And now, once discovered, he was told to wait.

"There is danger. Be careful. I will send you a message."

The man waved his arms again. This time a black hole formed and pushed towards him, engulfing him in its darkness.

***

Blake sat up in bed. Sweat dripped from his brow, his sheets damp with it. He struggled to control his breathing until his lungs began to find their normal rhythm. He looked around, trying to ground himself to reality, half expecting that he would wake into yet another dream or another room. That surreal feeling enveloped him, the dream clinging to his mind.

He blinked and stared at the clock on his nightstand. It read 5:00 PM in crimson digital. He'd only been asleep for thirty minutes but it felt like hours. For some reason, the time grounded him and he felt like he was back in reality. This was his real room, not a dream version of it.

The recurring dream had started out as usual, where he was the poet William Blake conversing with one dead soul or another. Those dreams often ended with him helping the searching soul with words of wisdom, or sitting and composing a poem based on the conversation. But this time it was different. In fact, the end sequence did not even feel like a dream; it had a much deeper sense of reality, starting with the extreme pain of the knife forced between his eyes. He rubbed at the spot, still feeling the pressure scar of that phantom blade.

He didn't recognize the older man with the limp. But he wanted to travel in the world the man had revealed. All his life he'd been searching for the mystical, had in fact made his living by narrating that search in books and speeches, but of late the journey had become flat, linear, and boring. He'd lost his passion for the quest, feeling like he was stuck in a rut and could not gain the momentum to escape.

Lying back down, he stared at the ceiling, hoping the rainbow portal would suddenly appear and suck him into its vortex of mystery. He needed something to make him believe again. Without it he didn't know whether there was much reason to go on.

He wondered whether his friend Martin had thoughts similar to this right before taking his life.

He shivered in the warmth of the room, picturing his friend's face. No matter how wide the smile, he now sees the sadness in those hazel eyes. Was his destiny to be similar? Would the frustration of always grasping for something slightly out of reach get the better of him, sour into depression and make him consider the suicide option?

He gazed over at the clock. 5:02 PM. The thirty-minute nap hadn't revived him and there was no time to give it a better shot. He needed to get up and start getting ready, or he'd be late for the book signing.

"Time to make the donuts," he told himself as he swung his legs out over the edge of the bed.

What he wouldn't give to be enthused about going to a book signing again. Now it was just something he was expected to do if he wanted to keep those checks rolling in. Somewhere along the way he'd lost his childish pleasure at being a writer. It was a dream he'd had to work very hard to realize. Now that dream, even after its transformation into reality—or maybe because of it—felt dead. He wished it could be different. But that led him to his other favorite saying: "Wishing so won't make it so."

For now he put one foot in front of the other, hoping that the next step would land on new turf. From there a new journey would begin.

He dressed and prepared to leave, all the while remembering the man's final promise: "I will send you a message." If there was any truth to dreams (and he believed there was), he hoped the man delivered his message soon, and he further hoped that he was open enough to hear it when it arrived.

If nothing else, he'd had a Blake dream, as he'd come to identify them, and not a nightmare of his mother's suicide. There was at least that to be thankful for.

***

Outside in the cold November air, his chariot awaited. New Jersey autumns were not as harsh as some, but Blake disliked the cold. His beat-up brown Toyota Corolla hatchback, sitting in its designated spot, shared its owner's opinions. Of the many things Blake had become uncertain of recently—career, relationships, life choices—whether the car would start on a cold night could be added to the list.

Putting the key in the ignition, he muttered promises of undying love to the steering wheel, running his hand gently over its gnarled surface as he turned the key. The engine whined, coughed, sputtered, and finally caught. "Attagirl," he whispered, patting the steering wheel, not feeling the least bit ridiculous in doing any of this, though he would not admit to himself the superstitious quality of the ritual.

He could afford to buy another car, but he took some perverse pleasure from inconsistency and the game itself. More than once he'd used the car as his excuse not to make some engagement or another. As he let the engine warm up, he contemplated that excuse now. He could walk back into the apartment, call Magix, and say his car wouldn't start— sorry, but no book signing tonight. But the truth was he needed to get out of the apartment, needed to be around other people before he became a real recluse. For being a recluse was one step closer to parting with reality, which was one step closer to full-on insanity. And he feared that more than he feared the small group of fans that would crowd around a folding table at the Soul Fly and ask him to sign their copies of The Deeper Dark.

It was the Mad Poet inside, with the strength of both nurture and nature behind it that he fought against. This dark ethereal persona slashed with razor claws at the deeper parts of his mind, cutting away reason while exposing the dark surrealistic dreams that made him question reality. It forced him to question whether he could differentiate the real from dream anymore. The belief that he could slip into a delusional fantasy world caused the fear he felt upon waking from sleep. Each time there was a moment where he couldn't tell what was real and what was dream, and wondered if he'd ever be able to truly distinguish them.

As he pictured Magix and Alma he realized that he was genuinely looking forward to seeing them. Small gifts. Another cross he could use to keep the demon of insanity at bay.

He shut his eyes for a moment. The rainbow portal winked at him, and he made a wish: "Let me see that other world and know that it is real." With that prayer he backed out of the parking space, turned right on Route 512, and started his journey towards the Soul Fly.

CHAPTER 3

Of all the things Romero hated about his job, the weekly Board meeting was the task he hated the most. It forced him to put on the corporate mask, bite his tongue, and clench his fists beneath the table as he struggled to remain silent despite his desire to add his sarcastic two cents to the conversation. The Board made him feel frustrated and beaten, their goals rarely aligning with his. He gathered up his presentation materials and glanced at the tumbler, tempted. Then he shook his head. *You're on your way to becoming an alcoholic. Don't give these assholes the satisfaction. That's all the excuse they'd need to throw your dinosaur ass back to the Jurassic period.*

Convinced, he left the office sober and walked down to the service elevator. He put his key in the lock next to the floor selection panel, turned it, and typed in his five-digit code before selecting floor A, the sub-basement. The elevator car lurched and descended. The doors opened into a dark area where storage cages sat full of cleaning supplies, bric-a-brac, the refuse of Strand-stolen inventions, and creations that had died on the vine. He passed these by and went to the end of the row, where another panel demanded his access code.

The door opened into the room Romero had dubbed the Strand Corp. Gift Shop. To him it was the most holy room in all of creation. The room reeked of aging paper, cured leather, dust and damp, combining to form that odor of ancient mysterious knowledge and promised revelation. What he loved most was its sharp contrast to the gleaming, antiseptic modern décor of the floors above. The room was draped in long shadows. A few bare bulbs glowed faintly, hanging from chains screwed into the stone block of the ceiling. It was not the bright hall of learning one might expect; it looked more like a dungeon or tomb. Shelves were carved into the walls, each stacked with scrolls and leather-bound volumes.

Here were the greatest intellectual and spiritual gifts of humankind. These works were so inspired, so revelatory, that they had transformed Romero's perception of the world, of truth, of reality. Here were the real miracles of creation.

When he'd first been given access to the room as a means of making his way to the lower catacombs, he'd had to get over the initial panic the room and its atmosphere had conjured. Being in the room flicked a switch in his mind that placed him back in the abusive closets of his childhood. He'd kept those memories chained to the darkest parts of his mind, a chasm meant to keep the monster from rising to the level of awareness. No matter how strong those chains were, the beast sometimes managed to scratch the surface of consciousness, unleashing not thoughts or visions—no, that would have been easy to deal with—but the experience of those nightmare worlds, the smell of sweat and fear, convulsion, fever, starvation, the anxious anticipation of humiliation and pain. In that moment he'd been transported back to his younger self: the closet walls closing in on him and choking him, his hands shaking, the distant shouts of his father, approaching footsteps reverberating through the walls of his prison and into his skull. He wanted to scream, to cry out, knowing even as he opened his mouth that there was no one to hear, no one to save him, not even God would protect him.

The first few trips through the room of treasures had him gasping for breath and grasping for the shelves to keep himself from falling. The panic attack was instantaneous, setting his heart pounding. He forced himself to breathe deeply and put the monster back in its cage. He felt sick and dizzy, but gradually the miracles replaced memory and now the atmosphere brought hope instead of fear—although now that too was beginning to dissipate.

The door at the other end of the room was the only reason most people came here. It was the only reason he was here now and was the only reason he'd been here for the past year. Thinking about that fact made him hate himself even more. Here were the true treasures of the Strands and he'd spent no time with them. Instead he spent all his hours keeping guard over the glitzy trinkets that passed for miracles.

He keyed in his security code a third time and heard the click of the lock. That click, or maybe what it represented, made his headache flare. Behind the steel door lay a dim circular staircase that lead into deeper darkness. "Christ," he muttered. Each step brought a deepening of the pain in his head.

The catacombs of Strand Corporation had been built by the founding members of the Strand Society. Their occult and philosophical treasures had come with them on the journey across the Atlantic. Upon reaching the new world and settling in Philadelphia, they had created an underground system of tunnels and caverns for the secreting away of both their society and what that society deemed important. First had been the library, or what he now called the Gift Shop, but then as war became imminent it was thought that further protection was needed. They had started digging and kept digging for the next fifty-plus years. No one knew all the tunnels. It was impossible. Romero was sure that there were still real treasures hidden in some dark crevice that had yet to be explored.

Next, they tasked Jonathan Tully with creating the Shadows. It was his oath that a person of his bloodline would protect the secrecy and sanctity of the Strand Society for as long as it was in existence. His family had been the spy and assassination arm of the Strand Society ever since.

With the beginning of the 19th century came new members with new ideals, and soon these members found a way to capitalize and monetize their knowledge of the Strands. Strand Corporation was born. And so began its legacy of exploitation of both the Strands and humanity. Down here, deep below the city that had given birth to democracy, was where Strand Corporation kept its secrets. It was where the true work was done. The shiny, technologically advanced halls and offices above were a façade. Above was where project managers, designers, and engineers built products, software, pharmaceuticals, and weapons. But down here was where the ideas for those were stolen. And now Strand Corp didn't even want to be involved in development. They wanted to steal ideas, patent them, and then sell the rights. They wanted to become a shop of thieves, completely removing any pretense at creation. In business terms they were focusing on their strength, which was theft. The founding fathers of The Strand Society would turn over in their graves if they were to observe the travesty built upon their ideals. It made Romero sick to have a part in such an antithesis. Like the slowly boiled frog, Romero had entered the tepid water of idealism and then the Board had slowly turned up the heat until it boiled with the credos of consumerism. Too late he realized the Board's objectives and by then he was too weak to jump from the roiling pot. He had become just another tool and he hated himself for it.

Romero reached the bottom step at last. His head hurt badly, the constant thump on the steps setting his teeth on edge. He reached into the breast pocket of his jacket, palmed three Tylenol, and slapped them into his mouth, forcing them down his dry throat. Fucking Board meetings.

At the bottom of the steps the worlds started to collide. The Board had had the main hallways of the catacombs tiled, modern lighting installed, and special rooms created for meetings and research. There were a series of clean rooms, surgical rooms, Shadow training facilities including a gun range, and of course the Conductor cube rooms. As he walked down the hallway toward the boardroom, he passed other tunnels that still displayed the original brick and mortar construction. These tunnels were still mostly unexplored. Any one of them could contain a Strand invention that could undo humanity.

He enjoyed thinking about this for some reason, a perverse thought experiment that ended with him saying, "I told you so!" while holding up his middle finger and waving it at the Board members. Someday some hapless visitor could take a wrong turn and uncover a black hole emitter. The jolly explorer would hit the big red button that says DO NOT TOUCH and the entire Earth would collapse into a singularity. Nothing. Gone.

He smiled at the thought, not really understanding why he found this so funny, especially since he would number among the dead. But he did. Yet even the chance of uncovering such a thing didn't give him the balls to explore. He could only picture a scene in which he was crawling on his hands and knees through the darkness, screaming for help, hopelessly lost. The architects had most likely created the insane complexity with this in mind, knowing that only the truly stout of heart would venture into unknown territory. Therefore, in all probability, the Doomsday Machine or the Kali Dance Disco Disk that lay hiding in this maze would never be uncovered, for the world was no longer producing the adventurer or stout of heart. At least not in his experience.

Two bodyguards stood in front of the boardroom door. They opened it as he approached and Romero could hear the drivel beyond. Christ. *There was a time when I was a neuropsychologist searching for the brain origin of spiritual experiences, and now here I am giving presentations on stolen patent ideas. I really do miss Alex.* The thought put him in an even fouler mood, if such a thing was possible.

He walked through the door into the Circle of Hell reserved for fools.

"Ah, Romero. Finally." The voice belonged to Thomas Agrippa, an angry man whose every word dripped sarcasm and venom.

"Hello all. Sorry I'm late." Even in his foul mood he was not in the mood for Thomas and didn't rise to his challenge, or rather, stoop to his level. Romero took his seat.

"Certainly is nice of you to join us. Must be difficult for a guy your age to make it down here on time. All those steps and all. Could someone remind me who it was that didn't want to install an elevator down here, arguing that he was afraid it might disturb some hidden catacombs and erase one of the mysteries of the universe." Thomas smirked, almost drooling.

There was a collective chuckle at Thomas's tormenting. All knew it was Romero the Relic who'd argued against the placement of an elevator. It was one of the few arguments he'd won.

Thomas was in the mood for a fight. "Who was it again?"

Romero was about to retort when Tim Farraday saved him. "Not now, Thomas."

Thomas swiveled to stare in Tim's direction, weighing him with his eyes. Tim was one of the few members of the board that Romero actually respected: tall and thickly muscled, strong in mind and body, and no pushover in any sense of the word. Even so, Thomas weighed his chances and seemed to decide that he could take the bigger man. His anger seethed, controlling his judgment. It was his Achilles heel and Romero was convinced it would be his eventual downfall.

Jim Farrell then gave himself up as a much easier target. In his nervousness he'd begun his arrhythmic finger tapping on the table, a habit inherited from his father, Jacob. Jim made the tapping even louder and more annoying when he took up his father's seat on the Board. At times it shook even Romero's calm. Thomas would tear him to shreds.

"Would you knock that shit off!" Thomas snapped.

Jim's eyes popped wide, his mouth hanging open, fingers pausing in mid tap. "Sorry," he said, shrugging his shoulder while moving his pudgy digits to his lap. A bead of sweat ran from the top of his bald head down the bridge of his nose and stopped on the swell of its bulbous tip, a crystalline pimple of fear waiting to be popped.

Spineless, thought Romero, as he contemplated punching Jim in the nose, his anger seething, needing a target. Blood had obviously not carried the strong character of father to son. Jacob had been courageous and intelligent, seeing quickly to the heart of matters. Jim was book-learned but lacked the passion or courage to do anything with it. If there was a week member of the Board, he was certainly it. Sometimes appointments made by heredity became disappointments. But as time went on, bloodlines died out. And even those rules were changing, appointments now being made based on perceived wealth, power, and business acumen.

As Romero surveyed the room he assessed each member and decided that only three or four were worth their weight. Even in business, most were stupid, and if they couldn't rely on Strand Corporation they would be out on the street.

Jill Grey, currently the only female member of the board, took advantage of the silence that followed in the wake of Thomas's rebuke. "Could we please finish with status so that we can all get back to work?"

There was a grumble of assent from the other eleven members.

"Jonathan, would you be so kind as to tell us if the Conductors, Watcher, or Shadow have anything new to report?"

She was the only person who called him by his first name. He could not recall when people had begun to call him Romero forsaking the use of his first name but he was convinced it was when the Board members had decided that Romero the Relic was a pithy nickname that conveyed their disdain for both his age and antiquated ideas. Jill had never stooped to the level of name calling and continued to call him Jonathan.

"Conductors have some projects in the infant phase, none of which are ready for filing."

Dave Collins interrupted from across the table. "Just to reiterate corporate strategy, projects are only being researched enough to get them to patent. We're not doing design or engineering research, or going down the path of creating anything, correct?"

Romero nodded.

"Steal it, patent it, and forget it." Thomas added with his patented sneer.

"The new credo?" Romero said under his breath, barely audible.

But Thomas, still looking for a fight, caught it. "You say something, Romero? Why don't you share it with the rest of the class so that we can all join in the joke?"

Romero grinned and he could almost see the time bomb in Thomas's head tick down. It was now one tick from zero. Romero had ordered the deaths of many, but none would please him more than ordering the death of this man.

Jill pushed her way back in. "And what of the Watcher?"

Romero answered without taking his eyes from Thomas. "There is some evidence to suggest that Alex may be helping Blake William."

That got the desired result. Everyone at the table was now staring at him. Alex, the Strand Corp. terrorist, had reared his infamous head.

"What evidence?"

"The Watcher believes he saw Alex enter one of William's dreams with the potential purpose of giving him a message or trying to make initial contact."

"You have sent Macaria to kill him?" Thomas pressed. "By him I mean William. He was put on the List a few weeks ago, if I'm not mistaken, and this further confirms why."

"No. I'm having the Watcher focus on him and have ordered the Shadow to follow him."

"Why?"

"Because William is the perfect recruit for Alex. A kindred spirit he could work with to get his ideas and agenda out there. William is a searcher and therefore doesn't really pose an immediate threat to the corporation. He could aid us in finding someone we have all been seeking for some time."

There was a communal grunt of approval at this.

"Very well. Proceed with your plan," Jill said after the briefest of pauses to assess his logic. "Anyone disagree," silence settled over the board room. "Good. Any last-minute items?"

"I would like to request again that the Board examine my proposal to have a new family take up the oath of the Shadows."

A collective sigh.

"Romero, we have voted on that," Dave said patiently. "The answer is no. The Shadows are no longer needed given our new corporate strategy."

"Were we not just talking about killing Blake William?"

"Yes, but only because we have a killer to hand. If we didn't have Macaria, we'd discredit him. Have him committed to an insane asylum, have the IRS put him in jail for tax evasion, use the Conductors to infiltrate his dreams and convince him of his own insanity or the stupidity of his ideas. These are much more creative solutions."

Romero did not like the way that Dave used Macaria's name. He always referred to her as the Shadow at times like this. As such, she wasn't the surrogate daughter he loved, the one he had raised, the only person he ever shared any of his thoughts and feeling with now that Alex was gone. But he let it go. Nor did he ask the obvious question: if these other solutions were so creative, why did they not use them now? For all he knew they were going behind his back, ordering the conductors to secretly run black operations. It would be difficult to run such operations without his knowledge, but not impossible. The Conductors, receiving orders from Jill or Thomas, could storm into his brain and change events or memories that would aid in hiding such activities. Maybe they were working William in parallel, driving him to question himself, driving him towards insanity. To them William was a piece of meat, a number on the List, and therefore deserving of whatever solution was convenient. They might also see him as a guinea pig for their new corporate stratagem, a way to determine whether they really could drive someone to the asylum or suicide. In the end maybe he was the mark, the rest just an elaborate play staged to misdirect him and ultimately lead him to question his sanity.

"Very well. I have nothing further to report."

***

He watched the rest of the members file out of the boardroom. Most had a zombie-like expression in their eyes as they calculated the millions they could steal. Just watching them walk down the corridor toward the stairs made his eye twitch. Finally Jill sauntered out. Her features were incapable of that blank look, her brown eyes intelligent and searching.

"Jill, I would just like to reiterate my request to continue the Shadow program."

"Why bring it up to me, Jonathan? You heard the Board's decision."

Romero needed to be careful here. He trusted her only because he had trusted her father, and that might not be reason enough. "Your father and his father had a credo. And that credo stated—"

"I don't want to hear about the credo my father and grandfather enforced as members of the Strand Society. I know about their philosophy, their history, the centuries of secrecy as they protected their hermetic and alchemical work, collecting the spiritual treasures of the ages, coming to this country to hope their enlightened occult ideals could take root in the fertile soil of revolution. I know it. I know—"

"Do you? Do you really know it?"

"The Board is right, Romero. Antiquated ideas for an antiquated age."

He didn't fail to notice the emphasis she placed on addressing him by his last name. She was showing her alignment with the Board and their ideals. The game was lost.

One last chance. "The credo stated that the Strand Society would—"

"I've heard enough, Romero. Please do not bring it up again." With that she turned to leave. Something stopped her and she turned back to him and placed a hand lightly on his shoulder while staring compassionately into his eyes.

"Jonathan, you have been of great service to this corporation throughout the years. That is why you are tolerated. But this is not the society it once was. This Board wants to grow fat on its cows, and if you get caught in their teeth while they are trying to enjoy their meal they will spit you out. Be careful and decide which battles are worth the price you will pay." She squeezed his shoulder gently, turned, and left, her heels clicking on the marble tiles as she made her way back to the circular staircase.

With the death of the last reverberation of those clicking heals the catacombs fell silent. This is when he enjoyed being in the catacombs the most. In a city as large as Philadelphia, with the hustle and bustle of life directly above him, he could stand here in complete silence, removed from it all. It was the only place in the city he knew that could provide the blanket of silence he'd longed for ever since he'd left the rural New Jersey town where he grew up.

He had only moved to Philadelphia because the Strand Corporation had hired him, in the dark days after he'd lost all hope of research funding by other means. The study of the effects of hallucinogens, particularly N,N-Dimethyltryptamine or DMT, on the pineal gland, and their relationship to spiritual revelation and near death experiences, was not a topic that had wallets flying open. In fact, it had more often than not landed him in hot water. But Strand Corp. was intrigued with his theories and his research and was willing to give him a large budget, private lab facilities, and willing test subjects. It was what he'd wanted at the time, so he thought.

As a new research associate he was not given the details regarding his test subjects or the true objectives of the program. He was told only that they were Strand Corp. employees that were interested in contributing to a study to determine if hallucinogens could increase their creative abilities. With such an unquantifiable goal there was limited success and he hypothesized to the Board that he may achieve better results if he could run employees through a training program that focused the hallucinogenic experience on more specific goals and tasks. He outlined a theoretical model for such training, relying on his previous research with DMT. It was soon after this proposal that the Board brought him into its inner circle, briefing him on the Conductors and their unique role in Strand Corp's business model.

Only the Board, the Shadows, the Conductors, and a few trusted others knew where the Strand Corporation's wealth of creativity originated. At the time Romero became an employee, the company had its hand in seemingly every industry, and analysts frequently tried and failed to learn the secret of its success. Where did it get all these ideas? What corporate culture did it cultivate to seed such a spirit of creativity and innovation? What Romero learned was that Strand Corp. did not succeed by inspiring creativity in its employees it robbed ideas from the thoughts and dreams of others and then sold them as their own.

There was detachment to his memory of these events now, twenty-five years later, but at the time he was in awe of the library, the catacombs, and the corporation's esoteric roots. He was told the history and given some background about the Strands and what the Strand Corporation did. It seemed surreal, even insane. He didn't believe it. And then he met a Conductor.

He shivered in the warmth of the catacombs, remembering. How wonderful his first experience of the Strands had been. It was so terrifying yet so amazing, similar to the explosive experience of DMT, but beyond it in every way. He remembered the pain of those ethereal fingers thumbing through his mind, the pressure and then the release as one dimension collapsed and another expanded. He was in a darkened room, staring into the eyes of the Conductor, and then he blinked and they stood in a dream world with lush trees and waterfalls and strange creatures drinking from a pool of crystal-clear water. He could hear birdsong in the trees, feel the humidity of the forest on his skin, smell the sweet aroma of fruit. It was as real as anything else he had ever experienced.

"Focus on me," the Conductor said. "Remember the room we left." He began waving his arm, drawing a circle in the air. "Picture the room in the center of this circle. Feel the cool air, the smell of antiseptic. Bring it all back." The circle grew opaque and then a picture of the room appeared. The circle moved closer or he moved closer to it, he couldn't tell, but suddenly it was engulfing his vision, folding around him. And just like that he was back.

"Fuck me."

"Indeed."

That was his first experience with Strand opening and traveling. Over the years he'd learned to travel without the help of a Conductor, but it was never easy for him. He had to have either drugs or a Conductor cube, and sometimes both. But just to know they existed, to know that what he saw of reality was merely what was contained on the tip of a pin, was epiphany enough. It changed his entire perception of the world.

He'd spent the next ten years training the Conductors, experimenting with various hallucinogens and methods to make their travels easier and loosen the knots of reality so that they could worm their way in and out of the Strands to steal the secrets that all people kept. He'd not thought of it that way then. Back then he had thought of it only as a project, a problem that needed a solution. He'd not thought of what he was providing or for whom, or what they would do with it. He'd forgotten the age-old adage of ethical scientists: "Just because you can doesn't mean you should."

And now, here he was, sitting atop the rotting corpse of the universe, protecting it from the rats and vultures that circled, hungry eyes seeking out a single morsel that once eaten would turn into poison and create an even deeper hunger. It made him wonder who and what he was really protecting. Was he in fact saving the vultures from the poisoned secrets that would ultimately kill them, or was he saving the Strands from the rats that would feed until stuffed with greed, tasting every miracle until there was nothing left but their bloated bellies and the resulting starvation?

He rubbed his temples. "Christ."

A cracking sound reverberated through the tunnels, disturbing his reverie. Was it a gunshot?

As he walked down the hall, he heard another shot and realized it was coming from the Shadow training facility. Macaria was undoubtedly pushing herself through some physical torment, as she often did. He stopped at the steel door and looked through the square window.

There she was. Black hair pulled back tightly in a ponytail, black halter, tight black stretch pants, a dark form moving across the floor. She was a beautiful woman, as she had been a beautiful child. She'd always been so loving towards him. She made him feel special, because to her everyone else in the world was a piece of meat, a potential target, but not him. She reserved any love she had for him and him alone. How could that not make one feel special?

She had set up a series of heavy bags, dummies, and paper targets. The heavy bags swiveled easily and had appendages that would whip around and try to attack the attacker. Deftly she moved through her self-designed gauntlet, flipping, punching, ducking, blocking. With each move she transformed herself—the snake, the monkey, the praying mantis—her muscles coiling and uncoiling in ecstatic sequence. It was a dance of violence. A gun appeared from nowhere: six lightning-fast shots downrange, six kills. Romero had barely registered the first shot when the gun was expertly holstered and the final test dummy had its appendages broken, the gauntlet completed.

She was crouching, silent, breathing deeply as if her display was nothing more than a stroll. No sweat, no panting, her heartbeat barely elevated. At that moment Jonathan Romero was proud. Proud of what she had become, proud that she was the best. She was death incarnate, a true shadow to life. She had spent her life in the pursuit of fulfilling the oath of being the best killer the world had ever seen, and she had succeeded. If there was any blame to be placed it was with him, for he'd directed the development and use of those talents. She could have been an athlete, a dancer, anything. And she would have been the best at those too. It was he that had created this shadow to life, just one more thing he'd corrupted as he'd lost his way. He loved her and regretted that he had ruined her life.

CHAPTer 4

The first thing Blake noticed when he walked through the large ironwood doors of what had once been a Catholic Church, was the music. Alma Vida and her band, Dark-Revelations, were on the Soul Fly stage, and the bone-crushing bass resonated in his chest as he made his way towards the back of the church in search of Magix.

The main hall, with its high ceilings, felt cavernous, its true dimensions hiding in dark shadow. Amber light cast from iron sconces danced upon the walls, each stone transformed into a glowing ember that pulsed with the music. This vast tunnel terminated at what had once been an altar but was now a stage. Red, orange and yellow lights played upon the performers rendering each into a twisting fluttering flame. Like many abandoned churches in Northern New Jersey, Saint Cecilia's had a dark past. The legend surrounding this church involved demons, devils, and deals. Magix had purchased it for next to nothing, as few wanted to invest in church property and fewer still wanted a building that was rumored to be haunted or cursed.

He'd named it the Soul Fly because he felt that it was a place where one could observe the soul of the world like a fly on the wall, insignificant but aspiring to be significant. This fly would live off the excrement of deity that the evolved left behind, eating the shit that would eventually allow the soul to fly free.

Magix was a strange man, schooled in many forms of the occult with a flair for the dramatic that at times was dangerous. He was a man without fear, who tempted and played with powers that were sometimes far beyond his understanding or control. Blake had played the part of savior on more than a few occasions.

Blake had no idea whether Magix was attempting to be trendy or a trend setter, or really didn't give a shit either way and just did what he wanted, but the Soul Fly was a success because of its eclectic feel. Magix often tried to help people he called illuminated artists, whether they were poets, painters, photographers, musicians, or writers. It was not uncommon to walk through the door and find an art exhibit, a local artist selling his work, or a poetry reading. Magix had also started a publishing company. There was an ever growing list of popular poets and novelists who'd started their career here one way or another.

Magix had published Blake's first book, and hosted his first signing at the Soul Fly. Blake would always remember the first time he scrawled his signature under his printed name. The ancient organic smell of the stone walls and the pine floors, the vague fluttering glow of the lights gave flight to mysterious shadows that held secrets creating an atmosphere that encouraged such nostalgia. The environment offered his senses those sights and smells that had been imprinted with so many of his memories that it was impossible to come here without reliving some event. Blake could honestly say that a large part of his identity was tied to the Soul Fly, either directly or through the relationships that had been forged here.

Magix also dabbled in music recording, and Dark-Revelations was the first band he'd worked with. Three of their albums had gone platinum, one of which was a concept album that was based on Blake's book A Mystic's Journal. Maybe it was Magix's clever matchmaking or maybe just providence, but Dark-Revelations' music and Blake's writing complemented each other perfectly, and in the process made Soul Fly Publishing and Soul Fly Records a ton of cash. As far as Blake could tell, that had never been Magix's intent. It was just a coincidental miracle. He didn't burn the money, but it never seemed to be all that important to him. That quality alone endeared him to many and especially to Blake.

There was really no central feature in the club. If anything could be considered central it was the stage. A few walls had been added to create cozy partitions or corners where people could talk intimately. In many cases these walls were specifically engineered to block sound from the stage. Behind the stage, a stained glass window depicted Saint Cecilia, the patron saint of music playing a viola. The altar had also been the place where a Catholic priest whose ghost now haunted the place had killed three altar boys before slitting his own throat, nearly decapitating himself in the process. The legends and stories, the play of light and shadow, the mysterious aromas, combined to give the Soul Fly the feel of a place where secret things could be revealed and discovered.

Blake made his way to the right rear of the church where the bar had been constructed. Magix was tending tonight, serving drinks and gossip in equal measure, as was his way.

"Usual, Mags," Blake yelled down the bar.

Magix turned and smiled. "Blake, my friend."

A glass of Diet Coke slid across the bar into Blake's waiting hand.

"That's it tonight, right, just the soda?"

Blake nodded. "Just the soda."

Like many artists and writers, Blake had experimented with alcohol to his detriment. He'd found that there was a demon waiting inside him, and once woken it had been difficult to control. At first alcohol had been a tool, but that tool quickly became addiction. It was the worst kind of possession, for there were few ways to exorcise that particular demon and fewer people still who survived the process.

Magix smiled and stretched out his hand. Blake took it, their handshake firm and committal.

"What have you got for me?" Magix asked with a grin.

"The Eye of Man, a little narrow orb closed up and dark, scarcely beholding the great light conversing with the Void."

"Hmm." Magix massaged his goatee, thinking. "I like it. Yours?"

"I wish. Nah, it's the other guy."

"That bother you? I mean, having that to live up to?"

"It was my father's idea of a joke. He thought it clever. It doesn't mean anything. You have a last name like William and your father likes William Blake so he thinks it's a great idea to name his son Blake. Nothing more than that."

"You sure? You ever ask him?"

Blake shook his head. "Didn't need to. My father found his salvation at the bottom of a bottle. He didn't understand William Blake any more than I do."

Magix pointed at the glass filled with Diet Coke. "Seems you tried searching in bad places for revelation yourself, if I remember."

"I know. You'd think after having lived with a schizophrenic mother and an alcoholic father I'd have known better."

"That wasn't my point." Magix paused as if he was waiting to see whether Blake could anticipate his direction. When no reply was forthcoming, he continued, "My point was that you know how it feels to be possessed by that same thing. Maybe you can let it go and give your dad a break."

"Maybe," Blake whispered, hoping that would be the end of it, that Magix would stop picking away at that scab and leave it to heal.

But Magix was focused on the stage, waving his hand at the drummer in a let's-get-it-going gesture and then raising his arms up in the air. There was thunder from the bass drum and then silence.

"Damn," Blake muttered, seeing Magix's game.

"Welcome, friends and fiends, lovers and losers, dreamers and despisers to the Soul Fly. Before me sits a great writer, named in reverse after one of the greatest mystical poets of all time. His songs are not of innocence or experience. He is neither a daughter of Albion or Son of Los. What he is, is the culmination of paradox; he is the marriage of heaven and hell. The wild heart, the crazy mystic, the dark genius, the Mad Poet. Fellow seekers and searchers, I give you—Blake William!"

Magix raised his hands, pumping his fists in the air. Alma screamed from the stage, venting some demon call that only her vocal cords could produce. The world exploded around him. Magix was nuts, crazy, but one thing was certain: he knew how to push people to new heights. If Magix had told him this was how this signing would go down, Blake definitely would have made an excuse for not coming, but as the cheering erupted all around him he felt like a part of a much larger organism. That violent energy tore through his heart and filled him with pride, hope, and love.

Before he even knew what he was doing, as if he'd become infected by the crowd, he stood, raised his arms, and screamed as loudly as he could. It was swallowed by the increase in volume from the crowd. For that one instant he felt like a god.

***

He signed the last book, looking up at the man he presumed was Seth, since that was the name he had been asked to inscribe. He was probably in his mid-twenties. Long hair, tattooed. "Thanks. I love this stuff. Made me look at life differently, you know. Changed my perspective."

Blake nodded. What could he add to that? Staring into Seth's eyes he saw himself ten years ago: searching for something, grasping for it. He'd left his father's house at 24, soon after finishing college. He just needed to get away. Get away from the memory of his mother and the alcohol-poisoned mind of this father. What he was looking for and what he would find, he had no idea, but he went searching. No matter where he went, what he learned, what guru or master he entrusted his spiritual growth to, there was something missing. It just didn't feel real for some reason. So he returned to New Jersey and took odd jobs just waiting for that something. That something that would make it all real.

The search and the questions it raised plagued him day and night. Not knowing what else to do, he attempted a form of literary exorcism. He wrote his journeys down, analyzing them in the context of his overall experience. Telling his own story of his travels and initiation into various occult groups seemed to lend a purpose to the quest. He began to add references and comments from other mystical, philosophical, or scientific works, as if he were commenting on the experiences of some other great mystic and savior and not himself. It helped him to concretize what he had felt, believed, and experienced. In the end the exercise aided him in elucidating what was important about what he'd learned from the various mystics and spiritual gurus he'd traveled with. Putting it all down on paper had a way of making it real, making it feel more important than it had before.

And that had been enough. At least that was what he told himself. But there was always something missing. It was that one missed spot on a painted wall, that glaring white swatch within a realm of relative perfection that caught your eyes every time you looked at it. No matter where it was, you found your eye seeking it out, honing in on it until it became the only thing that mattered. Why didn't someone cover it up, finish it? Take five fucking minutes and paint over it? Because it was the only important part of the wall, it was in fact what gave the wall any meaning at all. Yet at the same time focusing on that small imperfection caused increasing frustration and sadness, feelings that continued to build until they became overwhelming.

He continued to write, not knowing what else to do, and in these attempts he gained a new understanding of the insanity of artists and poets, for he felt the depression that came with frustration. Having visions, feelings, and experiences that spoke of a better and more beautiful world, but finding the tools he'd been born with were inadequate to express and share them, led him to a state of despair. Those rapturous experiences could not be framed or saved; they could be experienced for one holy instant and then were gone, their gossamer clouds evaporating slowly, haunting the mind of he who tried to give it form. As hard as an artist tried with paint or verse or song, they could not relive that moment. When reading the page, studying the painting, hearing the verse, one could only see, hear, and feel the lack, what was missing, the unspoken word that trailed each stanza, the empty space behind each oily figure, the silence shadowing each refrain.

That was the ache of the artists, their burden, the talisman and curse that hung from their necks every day of their lives, making them weary: seeing a world they could only vaguely share with others through their chosen art, knowing that even at the height of their greatness they offered the world only a mere phantom of the experience that inspired it. And Blake came to believe that the ineffectiveness of the body and its talents was part of the answer he sought; those eyes, those hands, had caged him. The tools that had forged his art at the same time forged the bars of his prison.

Seth pulled the book from Blake's grasp. He blinked. "Sorry. Spaced out for a minute." Blake shook his head to clear the cobwebs of memory.

"No worries. Thanks."

Blake watched Seth walk away, stretched his arms and legs, and decided to move to one of the central tables to listen to Dark-Revelations. They were probably a few songs from the end of the set and he wanted to talk with Alma before he left.

The stage was wrapped in darkness and silence for a moment. Then the bass drums beat softly, a tambourine came ever so soft, high hat, snare. A sitar crying for a lost lover, bass the thunderous heavenly reply, and finally the peal of lightning from the screaming six string guitar. And finally, when the crowd begged for it and the music would die without its contribution, there was the voice. It was at once angelic and demonic, speaking in the tongues of all men, a cacophony outside of this one ecstatic moment where all understood, where all were one, a slave to the primordial beat that resounded in each soul, engrained in one's being like spiritual DNA. In that moment, out of this disparate patchwork of styles and tones, the world was made whole. The music called the stars into alignment, angels bowed their heads, demons cried at the memory of the face of God, and humans—caught somewhere in between—aspired to reach the heavens.

Blake was drawn to its spell, the music touching him in a way few things could. It worked a special magic, a release, a spiritual evolution, filling his mind with bliss, tearing away at layers of illusions till it revealed the secret face beneath. The rhythm pulsed in his brain, his blood, his heart, making him feel electric. Its prophetic promise of secrets revealed and truths uncovered made him shiver.

The first time he'd ever heard technical or doom metal, he'd hated it. And then he'd met Alma and she had changed his entire outlook.

Their relationship had begun with them in awe of each other's abilities. When they met she'd told him that she loved the way he could put words together to form a picture in her mind or make her feel some emotion so strongly. He in turn could not comprehend her ability to make music. Blake had always loved classic rock and 80s metal, but Alma had given him deeper insight into what music was. When he listened to her he exploded with violent emotion and he learned the beauty of subtlety. Alma hammered the listener with dark booming minor-scale rhythms that at first he didn't understand. It all sounded the same to him—machine-gun double bass drum, power chord progressions, grunting, screaming—but Alma showed him that the genre's formula was only the base layer, the foundation for intricacies. Once she explained how to listen, the music opened up, and he found subtext and deeper meaning in each song and its various layers. She opened his ears and his heart to new ways of seeing and listening.

Alma had a way of always doing this for him, constantly challenging what he saw as ordinary, peeling back the layers and exposing the beautiful intricacies beneath. No other person head ever influenced him as deeply. Of course she said similar things about him, although he didn't see it. But they worked as best friends, finding something beautiful in each other that they could not see in themselves.

The song that roared from the stage now was titled "Neural Fire," and was one Blake knew well; it recounted the story of how he and Alma had met. Alma had a special form of synesthesia in which words or language formed tones in her mind. A story would then become a song. Her songs reversed this process and told a story. "Every song is a story that flashes images in my mind," she told him once. "It's like a movie going on behind my eyes. It's not exactly like that but that's the bests I can describe it in words. That's why I'm a musician. Words only make sense to me in music and music tells the story of my life and experiences."

Blake sat back, allowing the music to form images in his head. Dark-Revelations spun a magic spell that pulled the listener into the world they created. Blake closed his eyes, listening to each nuance, the sweeping arpeggio followed by a high-pitched harmonic scream, again, again, in rhythm, the music drawing him in. A void, an empty space, the world around him disappeared... and then came a soft whisper hidden within the shadow of the refrain. "Blake, listen carefully. We must meet."

A new world rose in front of him. He was standing in a desert and before him was the limping man from his dream. Behind him, far in the distance, a black tower loomed. "Blake, there is something I must show you before it's too late."

"Too late for what?"

"There is no time. Please trust me. What I have to show you you'll want to see." The man began to draw circles in the air with his arm again. Blake easily fell into the motion's hypnotic spell. "Meet me at the Haunted Peapack Monastery tomorrow at noon." With that a portal opened in the vortex created by his swinging arm and the darkness reached out and pulled him in.

The world slowly came back into focus as though Blake were a diver coming up from the ocean floor: the filtered light growing brighter, the aqueous haze transforming to clarity and bright sky. Blake shook his head slightly as if shaking water from his ears. Alma's voice bellowed the last lines of "Neural Fire" in Portuguese and then there was silence, the lights over the stage extinguished. Darkness.

Blake sat up in his seat. Did that just happen? Did it really happen? What the fuck is going on? Am I going crazy? Is this what happened to my mother? I can't tell what's real right now. Where my dreams end and where reality begins.

***

Alma came over to Blake's table and sat across from him.

"What did ya think?"

"Great."

"You don't look as if it was great. Your skin looks like ash. You OK?"

"Not sure. I've been having these weird dreams and visions recently." There was no one else he could share this with. Alma knew the story of his mother and the fear he had of becoming psychotic. For that reason, she was the only empathetic ear he had. They shared the bond of those who had stepped to the edge, nearly fallen, and somehow been pulled back.

He recounted the dream that he had had just hours before, and the experience that had occurred during "Neural Fire."

"Fucked up. But fucked up in a good way," Alma blurted.

"How do you figure?" he asked.

"There's an easy way to find out if it's real or not."

Blake just stared at her, waiting.

"You don't see it."

He shook his head.

"We just show up tomorrow at the fucking church. If he's there he's real. Pretty simple."

CHAPTER 5

Macaria took in a deep breath. The heavy bags were still swaying from their chains, the smell of gunsmoke and burnt powder wafting in the air. But she did not feel that calm of death, that ecstatic moment when all was silent, the violence subsiding, the reaper claiming his prize, she claiming hers. Her symphony was an ode to extinction, to blessed death. That was what she longed for, what her blood screamed for, death... death to all. In her dreams she saw herself as a shadow that hung over the Strands and her destiny was to destroy it all, to end the Strands themselves.

The door opened behind her and she quickly pivoted on the balls of her feet, the 9mm Berretta released from its holster and trained on the intruder in less time then it took him to realize what was happening. If she had fired he would have been dead before he'd even registered that she was moving.

"Fucking hell," Romero breathed.

She smiled, taking some small pleasure in the shocked expression he wore. Pride came in many forms. Holstering the gun, she walked towards him. "You surprised me."

"I don't think so."

"What brings you down here?"

"I was at the board meeting when I heard a shot and decided to come down and say hello." He looked away from her to the table where she had all her weapons laid out. Something caught his eye and he moved towards it. He picked up her Giger book, gave it a cursory examination, and then carefully placed it back on the table.

"H.R. Giger and metal music. Pick up any new hobbies?"

So this was daddy visiting her today, or at least for the moment. Their relationship was complicated but she allowed it to be what it was, knowing it was probably not any easier for him than it was for her. He confided in her about his cancer, his fear of dying, but she kept her secrets locked away. Her romance with death, the ecstasy she found in delivering it, and her dreams of ending the Strands were things she could not express. If the cancer took him to death's door she would carry him over the threshold. Moments before doing so she would tell him everything; she would relieve herself of that cherished secret so that he could take it with him into the next world. So that he could face death in peace. But not now. Not yet.

"Nope. Biomechanoids, demons, devils, and dark atmospheric doom metal. Everything a girl needs."

Macaria was no art critic, but to kill time one night before a mission, she'd gone to the H.R. Giger Museum in Geneva, Switzerland. She'd never heard of the artist, seen his art, or watched the Alien movies, but when Macaria walked through the gallery filled with visions of extraterrestrials, demons, ghouls, biohumanoids, and

Freudian mechanisexual landscapes, she came the closest she ever had to a religious experience. Something within the dark, twisted, metallic epithelial symbolism touched her in a way nothing else ever had. It was so primal, visceral, erotic. Like violence. Like death.

She lived a Spartan existence, but her small collection of personal possessions now included several Giger prints, all of his books, and the Bible, and she'd given up reading the Bible in adolescence. Relaxation was listening to the murderous atonal rhythms of her favorite death metal albums while losing herself in the darkly erotic and exotic world of Giger landscapes.

"Never got into Giger myself."

She wasn't surprised. Romero would only gaze into the darkness; he didn't want to walk in it. Growing tired of this game, if that was indeed what it was, she changed the subject. "So why are you really here?"

"I really did walk down to see you after I heard the gunshot."

For a moment she felt bad. Did he really care? She knew he did. But this whole thing of feigning interest in her life was out of character and furthermore it wasn't necessary. That wasn't what she needed. What she needed was someone who understood death and its beauty.

"But since we're both down here, maybe we can go check in on the Conductors and the Watcher?"

She searched his eyes. Now she couldn't tell which was true. Did he really come to say hi and just now thought of seeing the Conductors, or had that been his aim all along? Was he masking this subtle manipulation behind concern?

"If you have time," he added.

She shrugged. "Sure."

***

Romero led the way down the hall to the Conductor facilities. After keying in his password he opened the thick steel door slowly. The Conductor area was unique in that it was sound proofed from the outside. Other than HVAC ducts and piping, the steel door was the only entrance. The Conductors were not to be disturbed during their workings and they often preferred to work in silence.

Walking down a narrow corridor, they passed the Conductors' living quarters. There were red and green indicator lights to inform visitors which rooms were occupied. Three showed green, including the one for the Watcher, which meant there were three Conductors in cubes down the hall. Romero did not pause; his objective was obviously the cube room.

The door at this end of the corridor was sealed to protect the atmosphere of the room beyond. When Romero opened the door, Macaria felt the hot humid air rush past her. They both stepped in quickly, sealing the door behind them. The floor was tiled and for the most part looked like any gym locker room she'd ever seen except that it was dark, the only light coming from electric blue runway lights around the rims of the cubes and down the center of the aisle. There were also indicator lights above the entrances to the cubes. Three showed green.

Romero motioned for her to follow him to the left, where there was a soundproofed observation room fitted with a bench and a large Plexiglas window. He opened the door and they slipped inside.

"Let's wait a bit to see if any of the three emerge." Romero said once the door was sealed and they were sitting on the bench.

"Sure."

The cubes were sensory deprivation tanks. Inside each cube, a Conductor floated in body-temperature salt water. The objective was to clear all senses, which in turn would allow for heightened consciousness and increased focus, allowing each to perform their peculiar art unhindered. Beyond those steel doors, the Conductors were hacking dreams.

Many people could be taught to see the Strands through training or the use of drugs, but very few could become Conductors and manipulate them. A powerful Conductor could even force a group of people to experience a particular reality while excluding herself from it, so that the Conductor was invisible to them—delivering on the occult promise of a cloak of invisibility.

Macaria had visited the cubes herself. She could travel the Strands, but she could not easily shape the experiences of others, and her traveling was random. The Conductors could pick a reality to explore, people to follow, dreams to spy upon. With help and in a cube, she could do this, but it was taxing; she was not a natural.

Romero was fidgeting in his seat—uncomfortable with the silence, she surmised.

"You can't conduct, can you?" Macaria asked.

Romero shook his head. "Nope." He sighed. "I miss Alex. Watching him explore and expand the Strands was almost as good as being able to do it myself. Being in here always reminds me of him."

"No one has ever really told me why Alex left," Macaria said. "What happened?"

Romero paused and sat back. "Alex had different ideals, different goals. He was tired of using the Strands as a means of making money. Living off the bones of a dying world, he called it. Alex said that the Strands were like the spheres, or the sephiroth in the mystical tree of life. That each sphere was contained in a larger sphere and by breaking through from the inner to the outer you achieved a new perception of reality, a more complete view of the universe. It was Alex's belief that the Strands were the spiritual destiny of humanity, and that it was the job of the Conductors of Strand Corp to help humanity spiritually evolve." Another pause, another sigh. "The Board disagreed. Three weeks after that conversation, he left the corporation. That was ten years ago. And we've been hunting him ever since."

"What do you think? Do you believe he was right?"

"I don't know. And you?"

Macaria thought about it, and decided to tip her hand so as to gauge his reaction and see whether she could entrust him with the whole truth. "I believe that death is the doorway to enlightenment."

"Interesting idea."

She was about to tell him her secret when one of the cube doors opened. A human form emerged from the entryway. The salt residue and acid blue lighting made the scene surreal, as if some ghost were coming out into the moonlight. He glanced up at them and then came over and entered the booth. It was the Watcher.

"Hello, Romero. Macaria."

"Hello, Ben. Anything to report?"

"Yes, actually. I've focused all my watching on Blake William and I was able to intercept a message Alex sent him. William was told to meet him at the haunted monastery in Peapack, New Jersey."

"Do you know where that is?" Macaria asked.

Both shook their heads.

"But it shouldn't be difficult to uncover," Ben said. "There are probably not many haunted churches in rural Peapack, and even if we can't figure it out we can always follow William."

"Do you know when?"

"Tomorrow at noon."

"Very well. How long has Janet been in the cube?"

"Same as me. She should be out soon."

"Fine, I'll wait then. Thank you."

Macaria watched Romero lean forward, staring at Janet's cube. He began to bounce his right leg up and down, a habit that always identified his nervousness.

"You need to speak with Janet?"

"I've asked her to do something specific for me."

He didn't add and she didn't ask. She assumed the task would become apparent when Janet reported. They did not have to wait long. Within five minutes Janet's naked form emerged from her cube. Romero waved, beckoning her into the booth.

"Have you learned anything from the doctor?"

Janet nodded. "I don't believe his drug is going to work. He's been having terrible dreams in which he administers a shot to a number of rats that then die horribly, squealing in pain."

Romeo looked dejected but he didn't comment. Instead he got up. "Thank you," he said woodenly as he brushed past her.

Macaria followed him out into the brighter corridor. She could see the tension in his step. He was walking quickly, his fists clenched, his whole body coiled, needing to explode before it collapsed. By the time they entered the main hallway he was almost running.

"What is it?"

He didn't respond. Grimly, he yanked open the door to the Shadow training area. The door wasn't even closed when he began to yell. "Fuck! Fuck! FUUUUUUCK!!!" He overturned the weapons table and then ran over to the punching bags and began slamming his fists into them. His screams turned to grunts, then to tears.

Macaria ran over to him and caught him just as he was falling over.

She put his head in her lap, stroking his forehead. He looked up at her, pain and fear filling his eyes. She dabbed at the tears on his cheek. "That was my last hope," he whispered. "My last hope. There was an oncologist that was working on a wonder drug to shrink tumors so that they could become operable, specifically brain tumors. Last month he'd received the clearance from the FDA to begin animal trials. That is who I had Janet spying on." He took a few deeper breaths, trying to control his weeping.

"I don't want to die, Macaria. I'm afraid of what waits on the other side of that door for someone like me. Someone who's made a career of stealing other people's ideas and then having them killed. Someone who took a beautiful young girl and turned her into a killer." He gulped at the air before continuing.

"You know what I think about the most?"

She shook her head.

"The day the doctor gave me the news. He started off saying that the growth rate was slower than most tumors of its kind. I start to feel hope for a split second and then he puts his hand on my shoulder and gives me a gentle squeeze. He looks into my eyes and says, 'Your death will be painful and slow.' Why did he tell me like that? I've had nightmares about those words ever since. Did he see past me to my sin? I've lived in fear of death from that moment on. What I've feared more is that I won't be able to make it right before I die. Right for me, right for you, anyone."

He began to sob. She stroked his head. They whispered, in unison, "I'm sorry."

CHAPTER 6

Blake woke early and started a pot of coffee. Alma had spent the night so they could leave together to go to the monastery. He was grateful that she stayed because he didn't want to be alone. He couldn't pinpoint why, but the events of the past day had left him with a feeling of nervousness and generalized anxiety. A lonely apartment would have been the perfect place for such feelings to take root and flourish.

There could be tension between him and Alma at times, which he felt was most likely the result of not being able to completely define their relationship. They were best friends and loved each other. They had had sex on a few occasions, and at times he felt a sexual tension between them. They didn't seem to work as a couple for whatever reason. He almost felt that they had tried because that was what people did. But he was never sure why they worked as friends and not as lovers. With his friend Martin dead, his connection with Alma was the only meaningful relationship in his life, and he just wanted to be her friend if they couldn't be anything else.

Last night he had given her the bed and he slept fitfully on the couch, not being able to get rid of that feeling that he was going insane. Ever since his mother's death he'd feared insanity as if it were a communicable disease. There was research to say that there could be a genetic component, and at 30, Blake was still within the common age range for the onset of schizophrenia. Was that what was happening? Were these the early symptoms? Months from now, would he be in a white room, head bobbing back and forth, so many antipsychotic medications in his system that he drooled all over himself?

He took the silver pendant from his pocket. It was the size of a silver dollar and on its face was St. David of Wales standing on a raised mound of earth, a dove on his shoulder. The story was that a dove landed on the saint's shoulder as he was preaching and the ground rose beneath him so that he could be raised above the crowd. David was the patron saint of poets. His mother had told him that the medal would make him loquacious. Every time he looked at it he thought of her: her love, her belief, and ultimately her insanity.

"Morning."

Blake pushed the medallion back into his pocket. "Morning."

Alma filled a mug with dark coffee and sat. She was wearing one of his black concert T-shirts; it barely reached her thighs and left her black underwear exposed. He felt that tension in his heart, in his head, and between his legs. She seemed oblivious to it all.

"Thinking about your mother?"

"How'd you know?"

"I saw you looking at the medallion. I know you always think of her when you look at it or look at it whenever you're thinking of her."

"Yeah. I guess the past few days have got me thinking. Me being me, I'm always imagining the worst. Glass half empty."

She smiled at him and took a sip of her coffee. Her brown eyes contained flecks of gold that burned in the sunlight coming from the window above the kitchen table.

He smiled back. She had a way of filling his glass.

She pulled at the chain around her neck and revealed a golden cross. "See this? My dad gave it to me for my sixteenth birthday. Not sure why. He wasn't religious and obviously I'm not. I've often wondered why he chose this particular thing but at the end of the day it doesn't matter. I think he gave it to me because he knew that in a few years I'd be going off on my own and he wanted to give me something I could always have with me to remember him by. He died one month after giving it to me." She looked down at the cross. "Whenever I look at it I see his face and I remember how his beard would scratch my skin as he would kiss me good night, the smell of him... for one moment he's right there with me. That's what this is for me. It's not a cross, it's not a religious token, it's a blessed moment with my dad."

She put the cross back beneath her shirt. Her eyes are moist when she looks up at him, "There is nothing stupid about that. Nothing shameful in it. Hold onto it for as long as you can. It is something the world can never take from you no matter how cruel it gets. It is yours to keep and cherish."

***

A few hours later they were driving towards the haunted monastery in Peapack. There was no question about which monastery his limping hallucinatory friend was directing him to. Everyone in the area knew of the legend.

The story went that a group of Cistercian monks had opened the monastery. The Cistercians were a strange order, adhering to the vows of poverty, chastity, and austerity, but also one of silence. They spoke infrequently and only when it was absolutely necessary, such as at communal worship. Their life was one of meditation, prayer, gardening, and an esoteric form of martial arts taught to the order by its founders, who had been members of the warrior monk order of the Jesuits. The Peapack monks had lived there quietly for decades until one night one of the monks went insane and killed everyone in the monastery. Then he fled to the guest house at the southeast corner of the property, where he proceeded to torture, rape, and then murder a group of visiting nuns.

It was a bloody story of a bloody act, and it resulted in what ghost hunters termed a tumultuous poltergeist. Local teenagers and ghost hunters claimed that dead monks haunted the building, their silently screaming faces appeared in the walls (apparently their vow of silence followed them in death). Wailing screams came from the guest house, and blood ran down the dogwood trees that bloomed in the now wild garden.

The only difference between this supposed haunted site and others that Blake had visited or read about was that it was so active that few dared enter. There were actual police reports of trespassers who'd been beaten by ghostly members of the order, scared into psychosis, or raped by the ghost of the psychotic monk. These stories were enough to keep even the most stout non-believer or ghost hunter at bay.

When they pulled up to the gate, he was scared. Not of the stories or running into the ghost of the crazed monk, but scared that he would enter and there would be no one there, that this was all in his head. That he was becoming insane.

The gate was not well protected. The padlocked chain had enough slack that he and Alma could sidestep through. Hand in hand, they approached the entrance. There was a haunted feel to the air.

As much as Blake searched for revelation, it always terrified him. He feared what he would be on the other side. What new thing would he have to fear? Would he have to relinquish everything he'd ever loved? Would he notice the difference? Or maybe none of this was happening. Maybe it was all part of some internal psychotic episode and behind that door was a white-walled rubber room, nothing more.

They began walking up the steps to the main door. Blake prepared for the worst.

CHaPTer 7

Alex Tannersley stood on the tips of his toes so that he could glance out the small rectangular window at the top of the monastery's front door. The window had a good view down the stone staircase to the closed iron gates, the sidewalk, and the street beyond.

He'd heard the prophetic whispers on the Strands, a cryptic warning that told him that more than just Blake was coming. He did not know what to expect, but he was assured that he'd not misinterpreted the voices when he saw Macaria parking down the street.

Alex stayed on the tips of his toes for another moment, staring down at the road and the occasional pedestrian, his short left leg groaning under the effort. He hoped that whatever was coming wouldn't require much physical exertion or acumen. Stepping back and rubbing his hip, he tried to soothe the pain. He often mused over how the one-inch difference between his legs had modified the course of his life. One inch was responsible for him being right here at this moment, waiting for some monumental event—maybe one that would show him the purpose of his existence.

It was strange to think that every incremental choice had brought him, either by providence or will, to this exact place. That one inch had taken him away from sports and games and focused him on books. Interests in philosophy had led to physics and mathematics, which ultimately decided his career.

Then there had been the death of his elder brother. The football god, the popular one who'd attracted all the positive attention of his parents. His brother's one inch had been alcohol. One beer too many had made him a second too slow in turning his car away from the telephone pole that took his life.

Distraught by his brother's death, Alex had retreated further into seclusion. A need to make some sense of the incident led him to the new age section of the library, but the mystics and poets had nothing real to offer. Then there were LSD and alcohol, but these too offered little in the way of understanding. He turned back to physics, hoping that the mathematical surety of the universe would explain everything. It had not, but that didn't stop him from searching. It was the life of an inch. And that inch somehow led to Strand Corporation, working with Jonathan Romero, becoming a guerilla fighter in a war against Strand Corp and the Board, and ultimately to this moment, wondering what came next.

He glanced out the window again. This time there was some activity. A man and woman were walking hand in hand down the sidewalk. Alex recognized Blake, of course, and remembered Alma from the Soul Fly. After reading some of Blake's books, he'd decided to follow him for a time before contacting him, which had led to the Soul Fly, Dark-Revelations, and Alma. He wasn't sure why she was here but that didn't really matter now. What mattered was that Macaria was on the move, her body uncoiling like a viper, ready to strike. She moved so quickly and with such grace that it was difficult to perceive her motion as anything other than a dance that entranced him with its deadly beauty.

He was not a physical warrior, but he would do what he could. The time for action had come. His entire destiny decided in one inch. How odd.

He reached for the doorknob.

CHAPTER 8

There was not a white-walled rubber room beyond the door, nor was there a pleasant dream world filled with fairies and rainbows. Instead it opened into a nightmare. The front door exploded open, and the man Blake had seen in his dream was yelling at them to get inside as the door shredded into a haze of wood fragments and dust. In only a moment his world had become the scene of some demented thriller.

He pushed Alma through the door as he felt something cut across the top of his ear, a trickle of blood running down the lobe to his neck. He heard another bullet's hiss as it passed his ear, clipping Alma's left shoulder, spinning her around. Her terror-stricken eyes found his as he caught her. He kept his feet moving even when it felt like he was getting nowhere. He knew that their only hope of survival lay in getting through the doorway.

With all his will he held onto Alma and pushed forward through the fear. There was a terrible scream coming from somewhere behind him. Blake tripped and landed heavily on top of Alma, his feet still running through the air on impulse. She grunted as he rolled off of her.

"What the fuck was that?" she was screaming.

"Are you OK!" Blake held her face in his hands forcing her to look into his eyes. Her eyes were wild, chaotic, but did not look pained.

"Just a scratch."

"Come with me."

Both turned. For a moment they had forgotten their apparent savior, who'd closed and bolted the inner door, the outer doors beyond the foyer had been rendered to nothing more than wood fragments swinging from bullet pocked hinges. They could hear the bullets riddling the heavy iron wood inner door like a driving rain on a tin roof, and knew it was only a matter of time before it was turned into tatters.

"Who are you?"

"This is not the time, Blake."

Alma was already on her feet. Another question rose to Blake's lips and then died as the sound of the rain stopped. There was a heavy thud and then utter silence.

"RUN!" their savior screamed as he fled into the main entrance hall, circumventing a large desk as he weaved his way to a long, dark, narrow corridor. Alma was tugging at Blake, pulling him toward the corridor, but they only made it as far as the large antique desk when the grenade's explosion ripped through the vestibule. Wooden shreds from the door, now rendered into deadly projectiles, screamed through the air around them. The explosion did not knock him off his feet, but he felt its percussive force in his chest, almost knocking the wind from his lungs.

In most cases Blake was slow to react. In emergencies he was even worse. But Alma was with him and he wanted to protect her. The blast had shaken him into action. Reason was not his weapon here. Here adrenaline was king. He felt nothing as they ran down the darkened corridor, glancing over his shoulder to see whether their attacker was in pursuit.

Blake almost stopped in utter disbelief as he saw ghostly forms stirring in the monk's cells that were on either side of the corridor. With each passing second their wraithlike forms took on more flesh as they made their way down the hall. The ghost monks were kneeling at their individual altars, crossing themselves. Then they took up their warrior staffs and entered the hallway, falling in behind Blake as he passed. When they began to appear further down the corridor, Alma faltered; she'd not seen them in the rooms and was completely unprepared for their sudden appearance. The monks stood aside to let them pass, and knowing the urgency of the situation, Alma did not question the mystery. That would be for later, if there was a later.

As they passed, the monks flooded into the hallway, heading in the direction from which Blake and Alma had come, heading towards battle.

"Don't worry, they are here to help," the strange man yelled as he continued to sprint down the hall. "I just expanded the dimension they existed in before dying so that they could manifest here."

Blake didn't even bother trying to piece that knowledge together. Right now someone was trying to kill them and they needed to escape. Everything else would have to wait.

The man was opening the door at the end of the hall. It led to a small temple. More monks moved past them silently, their semi-solid forms moving at speed to join in the fight. Alma and Blake entered the temple, their new best friend closing the door behind them; there was no lock, no bolt. At the altar the man began waving his right arm in a circle, its motion hypnotic and now familiar to Blake. He heard the familiar sound of chimes followed by the whoosh of air: a dimensional seal broken, alien air spilling into his world.

Would he now get to explore the dimension from which that mystifying air emerged? The thought excited and terrified him. Even after the tumultuous events of the past thirty seconds, he hesitated, not sure that he wanted to get any closer to this miracle, for he had learned the lesson that there are things worse than death. The emptiness behind that hole in space could contain a world much darker than the one he lived in now. It could make him wish that the attacker's bullet had killed him instead of just grazing his ear; could make him wish that there was some solace to be found in death.

The hole appeared, the eye blinking open. It was a hole not just in space but in his entire conception of earth, the cosmos, reality, physics, religion; a taunting abyss that mocked all his petty theories and ideas.

Behind him he heard the sound of rain again as the door to the temple began to splinter. His mind cracked; he was losing it. How could any of this be happening?

"I just need to warn you that this is going to feel a little weird."

The portal eclipsed his vision, enveloping him, but this time there was no smooth transition from one scene to the next. The man was wrong: it felt a lot weird. His mind was ripped out of his head, flushed down a toilet, and then sent careening back into his skull. Nausea welled up in him as he experienced a warp in gravity, stretching him, threatening to tear him apart as each limb was pulled in a different direction.

Slowly the nausea cleared, as did his vision. There was a slapping noise. The world he saw, as though through a fisheye lens, was dead. The ground was a gray ash. There was another slap and this one hit him between the eyes, his vision refocusing.

He looked around him and saw Alma bent over at the waist, puking white bile into the sand. Next to her was the limping man. Blake shook his head. Alma stood up, wiping her mouth. "What the fuck just happened?"

Blake was still trying to piece together the events in his head. Everything had happened so fast. Nothing he had ever experienced explained this, explained where they were right now or how any of this was possible or real.

"My name is Alex and I'm here to help," the limping man said. "But I must explain as we walk."

"Help who, what? Blake, do you understand what the fuck is going on?"

"No, but this is the guy I saw in my dream and I think we should listen to him."

"But where are we going? Why do we have to walk anywhere? Look around. It's all dead."

"It's not all dead. There are two reasons we must get moving. One is because I have something to show you. It is why I brought you here. Two because the person sent to kill you will only be temporarily delayed by our escape into the Strands."

"Strands?"

"Yes. Strands. That is what this is called." He swings his arms in a circle as if to suggest more than just what they could see. "It is a term used to describe the system of the universe."

"What the fuck does that mean?" Alma demanded.

"I will explain, but please believe me, we have to move or we will die right here."

Blake takes Alma's hand. "I don't see another choice."

"Fine. Lead the way, then."

CHAPTER 9

Romero was waiting for her in the training room. He could see she was upset.

"Well, I found Alex and then lost the lot of them," she spat as she slammed the door behind her.

"What happened?"

Macaria efficiently and factually summarized her tracking of Blake to the Monastery. But when she began describing the events that transpired after she had breached the inner door the words spilled from her mouth in an angry stream.

"These fucking monks start appearing in the hall and at first I think they are some parlor trick illusion that Alex has set up to scare people away but as they approach they start to look more real. One of them takes a swing at me and I don't even move. I'm so sure this is bullshit that I just let it hit me and dislocate my shoulder."

She looks down at her feet, cursing. "Fucking stupid? I should have known better."

"Now that I know they are real I start firing at them but they keep coming and I don't know what to do. For the first time in a long time I don't know how to kill an enemy and it angers me. As the bullets hit I see a splash of substance or ectoplasm or whatever these things are made up of flying off of them. It seems my only chance and since I don't know what the hell else to do I lob a grenade into the center of the herd and jump behind the wall of the vestibule."

She paused to stare at Romero, wondering why none of this seemed to surprise or upset him the way it had her. "That did it. Whatever that shit was the grenade blast dispersed it and they were gone. But Alex's ghost warriors had done their job. By the time I got to the temple at the end of the hall I had just enough time to scream as I watched them disappear into the Strands."

Her knuckles are white, her hands balled into fists. "I try to pluck at the Strands but I can't find the tone. I'm too angry. I can't get control. All I can hear is my heart racing."

She begins to slap her one fist into the open palm of the other. "Gone! Escaped!"

"So I pop my shoulder back in and drag my sorry ass back here."

"Alex and his ghosts," Romero sighed. "What he does is expand the dimension in which they exist and somehow merge that dimension temporally with the one you perceive. I'm not sure how he does that and don't know of another Conductor that can, but he's used that particular talent in the past to get away."

Macaria hissed impatiently. "How do I find them?"

"We get a Conductor to find them and send you after them."

***

Two hours later, they were back in the Conductor Cube waiting area, waiting. Ben emerged from the tank and walked over to the observation room. "I found them. Alex has taken them to the Primordial Strand."

Macaria leaned forward. "What is that?" Romero turned to her. "The thought is that the Primordial Strand is the origin Strand, the one first created when the creator said 'Let there be light.' It is a dead dimension because it existed before choice and will created the rest of the system of the universe. Alex believed that at the end, or rather beginning, of this Strand exists the machinery of the universe. The place where the big bang occurred. The alpha of all that we perceive."

"Has a Conductor ever been sent there to explore?"

"They have. They've just never returned."

"Why?"

"No one knows."

"Ben, can you conduct me there?"

"Yes. But I won't be able to get you back out. Your only way out will be through."

Macaria looked confused, not knowing exactly what that meant, but she did not ask another question. She bit her bottom lip contemplatively. When the silence had stretched out, Romero spoke up.

"Can you leave us for a moment, Ben?"

Ben closed the door and Romero gazed into the eyes of his almost-daughter. "There is no reason to do this now, Macaria. Either they have escaped into a world they can't leave, or they are dead. Either way, the results are the same, as far as we're concerned."

"I'm not going to do this for Strand Corporation or you. This I do for me. It is the one thing I will ask of you, for all I have done for you and Strand Corp."

"Why?"

She put her hand on his cheek. "There is something I have always wanted to share with you but was afraid what you would think of me if I told you. But if this is the last time we will ever speak then I want you to know."

He shook his head, not sure what to expect. Was this the point where she told him how much she hated him, how she blamed him for the mess he'd made of her life and of the world at large? He'd deserve it but he couldn't take hearing it from her.

"I know you are afraid of death," Macaria said. "But death is beautiful. In all I have seen and done, the most alive I ever feel, the most alive I ever see others, is in the presence of death. When I share in that moment as I take another's life, I feel close to whatever it is that created everything. I feel part of life in a way that is revelatory. Whatever you believe, I tell you that death is but another door of life, one that few of us are courageous enough to face unless forced. But it is nothing to fear or run from."

She stroked his cheek. He didn't know what to think, what to say.

"Extinction is beautiful. I will either find the origin of life, the big bang, the house of God, or I will destroy it all, for I no longer see any point in any of this. And if I can't find it there then it doesn't exist to be found. I was born to bring extinction to the Strands."

He nodded, finally understanding that ecstatic look she got whenever death was the topic. He also now understood that she believed she was destined to end the Strands. The thought that this was typical psychotic delusion briefly crossed his mind, but he had seen too much to challenge her belief. She might very well be the goddess of death that she was named for. There was no doubt in his mind that she was capable of destroying the system. But complete annihilation scared him more than his singular lonely death. The death of all seemed too final.

"Whatever you do now, do because it is what you think is right," she added. "Don't do it out of fear."

The tumor twitched in response to remind him it was there. Did he have that courage? Was he even capable of making his own decisions anymore or had the tumor taken over? Was it now so large that it was pushing on his brain, tinging every action and thought with psychosis?

He wanted to be honest with her, especially if this was the last time they would ever speak. "I don't know that I'm capable of heroism anymore," he said finally. "All I can say is that you must go and do what you believe is right. That is where I lost my way and I never made it back. I should have followed Alex, joined him, but I let my fear control me and I'll regret it till the moment I die. Whatever you decide to do, know that I love you."

He kissed her forehead and saw a tear form in the corner of her eye. Even the goddess of death could be made to cry in such a world. But then again this insane world seemed to thrive on such occurrences of paradoxical irony, reveling in its ability to grow tragedy from the seeds of the sweetest flower.

***

Ben informed her that she did not need the chamber. He would pull the Strand and expose it to her, and she would have to let herself go and allow herself to be pulled into it.

Romero stood next to her. Part of him wanted to go with her, but he knew that not only did he not possess the courage, he would be a burden to her and might prevent her from completing what she feels she must.

"Are you ready?" Ben asked.

She looked at Romero. "I love you too." Looked at Ben. "Do it."

It happened quickly. One moment Ben was twirling his hand in the air, Macaria staring into the forming vortex. Then Romero felt a pressure in his ears, the tumor pulsing. Gone. In one instant gone, and with her the last attachment he has in this world, the last thing he truly cared about.

He walked away, now ready to face death in whatever form it took.

CHAPTER 10

"OK, we're walking, now would you mind explaining?" Alma asked.

Alex was walking quickly for someone with a limp, and already Blake was struggling to keep up. Alma didn't seem to be having any problems except that she was angry. She strode with arms tense at her sides, a spring coiling and waiting for release.

"What would you like to know first?"

"Well, I guess the most pressing thing first, which is: who is chasing us and why?" Blake cut in.

"Ahh. Good, that is an easy one. Money. Greed. The triumph of one group's ideas over another's. Power."

"Oh good, you cleared it right up," Alma threw back in her classic sarcastic tone.

Blake couldn't help but smirk. Alma had an issue with controlling her anger. Her favorite tool for expressing it was sarcasm. But it was the tip of the whip, and if Alex didn't start giving them answers, sarcasm would become outright violence.

"The person chasing us is what Strand Corporation calls a Shadow. She is the last of her breed and the most deadly, a very powerful and dangerous woman named Macaria. And she was ordered to kill you and me because we have been deemed dangerous enough to the ideals of Strand Corporation to be placed on the List."

Blake and Alma stopped and looked at each other. "Strand Corporation?"

Alex stopped. "Yes. You've heard of it?"

"Who hasn't heard of Strand Corporation?" Blake said. "But what do they have to do with any of this?"

"That, my friends, is a long story and we must keep moving so I will tell it as we walk."

Alex told them the history of the Strand Society, the birth of Strand Corporation, and their secret agenda. The story led to his involvement and to Romero: how they both thought that what they were doing was cutting-edge, that they were forging a way to expand people's minds to reveal the mysteries of the universe.

"My life goal had been to create a unified theory of spirituality and physics. But my ideas were slandered by my fellow physicists who couldn't seem to deal with the acclaim I received from my books on mystical physics. So they rallied together to dislodge this thorn from their collective sides by accusing me of using government funding for LSD and DMT research." He paused for a moment and sighed. He turned to face them. "Which I never did. But accusation proved to be enough. My funding was stripped and I became a full time author in search of some way to prove my theories, to show those that had stripped me of my dignity that I was right." He looked away and turned his gaze upward to the gray sky. His lip quivered slightly as he whispered, "Looking back now I see how wrong I was. My ego made me blind. I didn't stop to think what I was doing, or what Strand Corporation was doing with our work. Once I did, I ran and became the first Strand terrorist. And that is why they were looking for me."

He went silent continuing to shuffle through the sand, his shorter leg dragging slightly behind making a swishing sound in the sand with each step.

"So this Strand thing—" Blake began.

Alex rolled his head in a circle attempting to remove the knot forming in his neck before answering." The people who first started the Strand Society used metaphors to try and explain the structure of the universe, and the one that seemed most popular is that of an intricately woven carpet. When you step back and look at the carpet you see a pattern or a picture, when you get closer you see the individual strands. If you were to pull one of those strands and start to unravel it you would reveal more strands; then if you were to take one of those strands and look at it closely with a microscope you'd see more intricacy again, and on and on. What we see most often is one of the Strands. There are other threads running parallel and perpendicular to them or even interwoven but we can only perceive one. Choice, creativity, and dreams create tributaries and alternate dimensions that continue to unfold in the system of the Strands. We perceive choice as doing either this or that and once we make that choice we feel it is done. But how our life would proceed with that alternate choice continues as another tributary, another split. Think of how many choices you make in a day and then multiply that by the billions of people. The Strands were so called because of this analogy. However, I don't think it tells the whole story because it doesn't give an appreciation for the hierarchy or levels of reality. Even though these alternate dimensions will often appear as filaments or fibers that is just perception. There are increasing degrees of truth as you move higher up the ladder of perception."

"What analogy does tell the whole story?" Alma asked.

"In one of my books, Physics, Immortality, and Mysticism, I used a different thought picture that I prefer."

"The spheres?"

Alex glanced at Blake. "You've read it."

Blake nods. "But that was written by Darren Romanowsky, along with a few other physics books like it."

"Yes, one of my pen names used to keep Strand Corporation from knowing that I was publishing. But that's good, that will make this a little easier. I like to think of each dimension as a sphere and that sphere can be contracted or expanded and the mind has to choose which it sees. One of the earliest theories that Romero and I came up with was that the mind's neural circuits were normally wired to perceive only one sphere at a time. So when the mind chose to see one it was at the abandonment of all others. Drugs, sensory deprivation, occult practices, messed with that neural circuitry in such a way that a person could loosen that rule temporarily and merge or expand multiple spheres at once. The ancient members of the Strand Society used many occult rituals or meditative practices that were specifically devised to change the vibration patterns of neural and biochemical circuitry, resulting in the expansion of perception."

Alma asked, "So they would willfully modify their brain chemistry which would allow them to pick and choose the spheres they could see. Correct?" Alex nodded. "But then how is it that we often perceive the same dimension?"

"What we collectively call normal reality is an agreed-upon dimension that shares a certain frequency or uses human standard neural circuitry; it's our perceptual DNA. Our minds are hardwired to agree on which sphere we collectively agree to call reality. That is what society at large has termed the real world to the exclusion of all other possibilities. Consensual reality is, in that case, the main sphere or Strand. Psychosis, hallucinations, and dreams cause neural rewiring that temporarily or permanently changes the switches in the brain and allows for the experience of other dimensions."

"Now think of all these spheres interconnected in all dimensions, and then imagine all these smaller spheres contained in larger spheres and so on and so on. Each larger sphere contains a more complete picture of reality, a higher order of reality. You follow?"

They both nodded.

He then moved on to the Conductors, explaining how they could control others' perception of the Strands and collapse and expand dimensions that were perceived by others. And finally he arrived at explaining the Primordial Strand they were on and why they were on it.

"I've read your books, Blake, and I saw you as being open to the Strands. For that reason, I wanted to show them to you. There is something else I want you to see and once you see it I'll let you decide what you want to do from there. But I chose you because you are a poet and a writer. I've struggled over the last ten years since leaving Strand Corp with the words to describe this place, the beauty of it, the rapture it can inspire."

Blake was confused. He felt like he should be a lot more freaked out by being in an alternate dimension on some weird backpacking trip through a desert that did not contain any life or color because they hadn't been created yet. The sky, the sand, his skin, Alma, this entire world lacked color and distinction; it was as if he viewed the world through a gray filter. There was no sharp contrast between black and white, lines blurring as if some poisonous bland vapor enveloped them. The air he breathed was tasteless and carried no echo or embellishment to their voices. It was a foggy banal limbo devoid of those sights, sounds and feeling that he previously used to classify rainbow reality with its myriad sensations. All of this should make him question his perception. But he wasn't. Was that part of being insane? Not questioning reality anymore? Not questioning why he didn't feel hunger or thirst in a desert devoid of moisture or food? Why he, a lifelong pessimist, wasn't worried about dehydration or starvation? Or why the ash felt inconsequential, a cloud of dust that he would drop through when he took the next step. Another thought which should have concerned him but didn't. He'd always felt there was more to life than what he could see, but he had no idea it was this. His whole life had been spent in the pursuit of truth, in search of revelation, and here it was. Those other journeys had been mere preparation for this one. And maybe that was why he could accept it. No matter how dreamlike this world looked and felt he knew it was real. He looked over at Alma and saw that same acceptance. They'd walked many of the same paths together.

"Alma, you are a welcome addition. I've always loved Dark-Revelations. And like most people, I became acquainted with Blake through your music and the songs that told his stories. Like Blake I'm sure you could paint a far better picture of this place than I can.

I can't separate my scientific mind from this no matter how hard I try. I see the possibilities for spiritual revelation and evolution, but I can't experience them or share them. For the past ten years I've been taking artists, musicians, and spiritual gurus here with the hope that they could bring back with them the promise of a better world."

"So where are you taking us?"

"A place called Damcar. It is a small piece of the universe that sits in a pocket in the Strands. Out of time, you might say. It is beyond the misty veil. And then beyond Damcar is the Tower, where I believe the machinery of the universe exists. I believe it is what set all this in motion: the big bang, the loom, the giant bubble maker, what have you. But no more questions now. The Geburiak will be much more equipped to answer your questions than I."

Blake could have asked a million questions, starting with what was a Geburiak, but he felt it better to wait. He already had a lot of information to chew on.

He took Alma's hand as they walked. "You OK with all this?"

"Not sure. Not sure I even believe it's real yet. It doesn't feel like a dream, except for the fact that when I look around it seems like I'm stuck in some weird blurry black and white photo, but at the same time I can't believe that my mind would just accept all this."

He'd just been thinking something similar. "Maybe something in us just accepts it as true. The rest is just putting one foot in front of the other and seeing what happens."

She nodded and smiled. "Yeah. I get that." She paused. "We've seen a lot together you and me, been through a lot."

"Quite a bit."

"I'll never forget what you did for me in Peru. Whatever happens, I just wanted you to know that you did more than just save my life that day. You changed it and gave it a purpose."

"You changed mine."

"I don't know where this journey is going but I'm glad we're doing it together."

She squeezed his hand and he knew in that moment that he loved her.

***

Alex sat down on the sand and rubbed his left hip. "Sorry I had to stop."

"What's wrong with your leg, injury?"

"Genetics. One leg shorter than the other. That's why I'm a science nerd. Walking like this sure makes it hurt though. Seems even salvation is a young man's game nowadays. Makes me wish I was back in the lab."

"No you don't."

Alex smirked. "All right, you got me. Just give me a few minutes and I'll be good to go."

The worst part about stopping was it made Blake realize how dead the air was. No breeze, no sound, no birds or insects of any kind—the world was completely silent. Blake had been to Maui and had hiked the Mulakini Crater rim trail, which rose to 14,000 feet and then descended into hot humid rainforest. At the top, in the shadow of the peak, the crushed lava underfoot and thin sulfurous air combined to form an environment devoid of all life save a plant called silver sword that bloomed for only short periods of time; their white skin reflecting the sun's rays making them look like swords rising from the ground. During that hike he had learned what true silence was. He'd been by himself with twelve miles of desolation to keep him company. It was eerie. He didn't know there were places so silent. It occurred to him that all life made noise. Even there on the crater, if he were to stand completely still his breathing made a deafening noise, the pulse of his heart booming in his ears. Silence was akin to death.

This world was more silent than that and he had not found the equivalent of a silver sword to make him hope for any form of life. Even the sound of his breathing and the beat of his heart seemed to be swallowed up by the air that surrounded them. All had been silent in this world till now. Now if he listened carefully he could hear a hum—no, not exactly a hum. He tried to find a word for a thousand different voices humming and babbling like a cacophonous psychotic stream. A warble.

"I'm starting to hear something." Blake said.

"Like millions of mumbling voices?" Alex asked.

Blake focused. He could see Alma concentrating. "Exactly."

"We are getting close to the Veil. Help me up and we'll get going. Just one more inch to go."

***

After another mile or so of walking they crested a dune and Blake gasped.

"Holy shit."

"Yeah. That's the usual reaction. That is what I called the Veil."

"I pictured smoke or vapor, not this."

The mist or wall was mercurial, reflecting the landscape before them, its surface bubbling and shifting, warping the reflections. There were actually two walls, stretching from distant points on the horizon to meet at right angles not far from where they stood.

"What is behind it?"

"Look over it."

Blake had been so focused on the wall that he hadn't realized it was only about 50 feet high, and he could see over it from their vantage point on the dune. What was directly behind it was hidden, but he could see a swirling tempest of colors in the distance that coalesced around a black tower. The tower glowed with a strange light. Its surface seemed to shimmer, as if it were made of onyx or dark glass that captured light. The top of the black spire was hidden by dark clouds, but directly below the clouds was a balcony. Blake squinted, thinking he saw a figure there gazing in their direction. A robe or cape fluttered in the wind. Then it was gone.

"That point where it looks like a whole bunch of rainbows crash together is called the Nexus."

Blake stared at the junction that Alex pointed out.

"It is the point where the Strands come together in a tight knot. From there," he moved his arm up tracing the multicolored path of the Strands from the Nexus to the tower, "they proceed into the tower which is the Alpha and Omega of the Strands."

Blake was awed by the sight. The tower pulsed with the river of color that flooded into the huge archway at its base. From this vantage point the Strands appeared to Blake as millions of fiber optic cables twisted together to form a rope of color and then entered the tower which was ominous in scale and one of the largest structures he had ever seen. He estimated it would take many hours to either circle it or climb it.

"It's like the whole world is spinning around it," Alma said.

Blake looked again at the spire and the formation of the clouds. She was right. All of a sudden he felt as if he were swirling, caught in the grip of a whirlpool, circling towards the crushing epicenter. Being hungry and tired, he was not sure how much he could rely on his senses, but he felt it all the same. The orbit of their bodies and those of the clouds (maybe even that of the entire universe) was not around the tower but felt more as if it was because of it, as if the spire was the cause of the motion and not its terminus. The clouds rotated clockwise, the sand a constant wave that moved in the same direction as if being turned by the force of the tower. The motion was slight but perceptible if you looked for it.

At that moment a feeling arose in Blake, a need; he wanted to be in that tower. It was a machine of the Universe. It was the energy that powered the Strands. If he could, he wanted to climb to the top to see if he could also speak with its occupant—if indeed his eyes hadn't been playing tricks on him. What would he ask of such a being?

Blake took a deep breath. He'd been on this journey for a lifetime, and he wondered whether he wanted it to end. Strange. What would he be afterwards? If he was no longer the questing knight, would he be stripped of his weapons, his armor? And what lay beyond? Was there a life once the grail was obtained?

"Right behind the wall is the village of Damcar. I've never seen it so I don't know what to tell you to expect. I have always believed that any place that sits between the Veil and the Nexus must be stunning. I have no proof but I've always imagined it to be a place of sublime beauty; colorful, surreal, revelatory. I believed that the tower is the beginning of the universe because it is where the Strands begin and end. The place where God lived." Alex paused, looking for words. "The space between the wall and the Nexus is... let's call it a pocket out of the system. It does not completely belong in the Strands. It is an abyss between worlds."

"You said you couldn't tell us what to expect?" Alma asked. "But you've brought others here, you said."

Alex hesitated, looking uneasy.

"Just spit it out," Alma snapped.

"I've never been beyond the wall," he admitted. "I've sent others beyond but they have never returned. Maybe they go on; maybe they stay in Damcar. I don't know."

"But you said we'd have a choice." Alma looked confused.

"You do. I'm not saying you have to go through the Veil, but I can't tell you what is beyond it or what you'll find. Stepping through that Veil is like dying. There are stories, theories, people who have said they've been to the other side and then come back to tell the tale, but none of it can be proven."

"I don't understand," Blake said. "You said you chose me because I was a poet. What difference does it make what I was if I go beyond the Veil?"

"I don't know that it does. My belief is that beyond that Veil is a world that can't be explained with logic and science. It is a world of miracles and art. A world that could only be described by a poet or artist. What I said is, I don't know if anyone has ever come back. That doesn't mean they haven't. Maybe they change their names and keep their story secret or hidden by cryptic hermetic language so as to avoid scrutiny, rubber rooms, and the shame society heaps on the visionaries. Maybe they become born in new bodies. Maybe they cross over into another world. What I do know is that I've read things by poets and writers that make me believe they have seen what is on the other side of that wall. They use words to make me feel something I'd never felt before, make me experience things I couldn't have understood before. Maybe all the truly great works—those works that allow us to travel in new worlds, taste new flavors, find new loves, feel at one with all things—were created by those who've taken a trip beyond. For all I know, you know, you've both been beyond the Veil before and now you're back for a refresher."

"I'm in."

Blake stared at Alma. "You don't even want to think about it."

"What's to think about? One foot in front of the other, right?"

Blake shrugged. "Right."

"Well that was easy. Since I'm not going with you, there are just a few things I think you should know, and then I'll take you as far as the Veil." Alex sat, rubbing his hip again. Alma and Blake joined him, forming a small sitting circle in the sand.

"This is more of a lesson. Maybe it will help; maybe it won't. I chose the people I brought here based on a belief that the system of the Strands is self-healing. Its method of self-healing is to use the creative intelligence of those who exist within the system to make changes that affect the entire system. There are two concepts I've tried to explain in my books that point to this, soul types and phase states. Soul types is a philosophical concept coined by Plato and phase states is a particle physics term."

Blake tried to pay attention, but his gaze kept drifting to the shimmering wall and the tower balcony hoping to catch another glimpse of the figure he had seen there. Alma sighed and sifted sand through her fingers wanting to take action and run through the Veil.

"Physics at its core is bent toward reductionism," Alex said. "So we try to quantify just about everything. We're like the baseball fans of nature, except we try to keep every useless statistic, not just RBIs and batting averages. So in that vein, if a human has so many cells, so many neurons, and we compute the possible states of all these units and multiply these along with all the conceivable combinations of each of these states, we end up a with a number, a very large number that quantifies human experience. A number that does not go to infinity is, by definition, finite. That number basically puts a limit on human experience. No matter how many lives we may live, in a closed universe such as this one, there are only a finite number of possible quantum states for a human being to be in. That makes him, in computational terminology, a finite state machine." Alex paused, seeing both Blake and Alma poised to argue. "I know this is hard for you to accept. We all want to believe we are unbound, completely free, and I believe that is true, but only under very specific conditions, which I'll get to later. I'd just ask that for the time being you keep an open mind."

They both nodded.

"That means that with enough time, we are bound to repeat the same state. There are two conclusions to this theory that fit this situation. One, that in a closed universe, because of the limit on possible quantum states of a finite state machine, there are a finite, although very large, number of multi-dimensional possibilities or Strands. Second, I believe that both of you are a quantum reoccurrence of a particular state. That concept then leads us to soul types. You with me so far?"

Blake was. He was glad he'd read a few of Alex's books or he'd be hopelessly lost by now.

Alma, who had always been smarter and quicker, was nodding her head as well. "So far so good."

"Good! Now Plato believed there were certain soul types. Even though he never explicitly stated it, Plato had reduced the concept of man to that of a finite state machine and his theoretical soul types were a reoccurrence of a particular state embodied by particular souls or spirits. You may experience memories of other lives, other worlds, but in truth they are all one. They are the same quantum state reoccurring, a soul type that manifests itself through the laws of physics."

"And what are our soul types?"

"You," his eyes moved between Alma and Blake, "are the sages, the prophets, the poets, spiritual revolutionaries, and saviors. You are the ones who lead others to an awakening, a new understanding. You are the re-occurrence of Gilgamesh, Osiris, Jesus, Buddha—the Redeemer. That is your soul type. I don't think I chose you as much as the system of the Strands revealed you to me. The Strands are calling you home."

He paused. Neither said anything. There was a shocked silence.

"OK. I know it's a lot. One last thing. This one is more of a warning. Things get a little weird as we get closer to the Veil and may get even weirder beyond."

"Describe weirder," Blake said dryly. "Anything like curiouser and curiouser?"

"Quite a lot, actually. As we get closer to the Nexus the Strands get closer together. Being that you are not traveling in a particular Strand but between them, you may encounter multiple Strands simultaneously, which is a condition I told you previously your minds are not wired to grasp. So just take them as surrealist images; try not to fear, understand, or fight them. Time may also loop a little because the intertwining of strands may cause the future to occur before the past and your experience of the present will necessarily be warped."

"That sounds like a lot of fun," Alma said. "Thanks for the warning."

Blake couldn't help smiling. "Is that it?"

"From me or her?" Alex asked.

"Both. Either. Neither."

"I'm good," Alma answered, smirking.

"Then so am I."

They stood and began their walk towards the distant Veil.

CHAPTER 11

Macaria had traveled the Strands before as a Conductor, but it had never felt like this. It felt like being in the center of a tornado: arms and legs pulled in different directions, brain slamming against her skull, ears popping, stomach lurching. When the ride stopped, she threw up in the sand.

Surveying the landscape, she saw only sand and sky in all directions. Everything was dull gray, dead and lifeless, an out of focus black-and-white photograph of an endless desert. As she surveyed the surroundings, her keen eyes found the footprints of the trio that had gone before her. Ben had been exact, unless this was the only place you could enter this particular Strand—but she thought not. Whether Ben was expert or lucky didn't matter, she saw her path. Time was strange in alternate Strands, so it couldn't be completely relied upon, but calculating the drive back to Strand Corporation from the monastery, her report to Romero, and then the time it took for Ben to find her quarry and send her here, she estimated that they had about six or seven hours' lead. Since she could run for at least two hours and Alex could only limp along, she was sure she could close the gap in short order.

She strung the large-caliber sniper rifle across her back and hung the AK-47 assault rifle across her chest, placing one hand on the stock so that it wouldn't bounce as she ran. Then she was off.

As she jogged, she noticed the strange quality of the air. It did not seem to carry sound. It wasn't just that there were no external noises, but even her breathing, the shifting of her clothes and the guns, barely made any noise, as if the air dulled the intensity of sound waves. It was a strange experience, like being in one of the Conductor cubes, knowing that you were moving and breathing but unable to experience the result of it. It was strange but she liked it. Silence. Blessed silence.

An hour later she crested a dune and saw her targets disappearing over another dune in the distance. She'd made up the time even faster than she thought. Another mile or two at most, she calculated. She ran on but slowed her pace as she reached the top of the dune she had seen them crossing.

Peeking over the top, she froze. Even for an assassin used to making split decisions in complex situations, what she saw was too much to make sense of all at once.

First her eyes zeroed in on her three marks, who were about a quarter-mile distant. They were walking towards a silver wall that shifted and undulated like a bubbling cauldron. A strange cacophony arose from it. This was the first sound she had encountered and maybe the only one this Strand did not, or could not swallow. Beyond it, in the distance, was a black tower rising through the clouds, surrounded by a swirl of colors that could only be the

Strands themselves. Her eagle eyes picked out the black-clad figure standing on a balcony studying the scene.

Immediately her imagination conjured up Gigeresque images of aliens and biomechanoids. It was a world he would have created, the tower a giant phallus exploding from the gray ash, up through the myriad complexity of the rainbow-colored Strands, and penetrating the clouds that splayed like dark phantom legs, waiting for the eruption of light that would spill from the tower when it reached its climax. This world was a complex colossus, the Veil separating the torso from the private regions where the generative organ rose and prepared to spill its rapture into the holy mother. It was an awe-inspiring sight.

More pressing than all the wonder on display behind the Veil was the activity taking place before it. A dark twisting cloud rose from the ground and started approaching the trio. She realized with tingling revulsion that it was a sandstorm made of worms.

Suddenly she noticed movement to her right. She spun and aimed the AK directly at the motion, waiting to see what horror would reveal itself. Something was burrowing towards her, pushing the sand up into a sand snake whose head was directed at her. Her finger was poised on the trigger.

Two beady eyes erupted from the sand, staring at her. When she didn't fire, the rest of the creature emerged slowly from its sandy blanket. Its body was covered in thick, blood-red scales. It had the tail of a lobster but the flat oval torso of a crab, and its eyes swiveled on two antennas. More eyes telescoped from the sand, staring at her.

The original member of this strange club opened up its mouth. The mouth gaped so large that she thought its entire torso might rip open to expose sharp metallic teeth, hundreds of pointy needles in rows and columns covering every available inch of its mouth and throat.

It opened and closed this wide jaw, its teeth creating a ringing chime that was not unpleasant to Macaria's ears. It was the sound of clashing swords, the bolt of a rifle sliding into place, the music of violence. Rising to its call, hundreds of the crimson creatures emerge from the sand all around her, each picking up the tune of the one before until their collective song formed a hymn of worship to Lord Death. The sound hypnotized her.

Behind the clashing and gnashing of teeth she could hear a whisper that arose from inside her head, as if the speaker had wormed its way into her mind. "Shadow. Kali. Thanatos, Reaper, Hades, Macaria. You have had many names, many forms, and we have waited for your gift of Blessed Death."

With that, the sounds stopped. She shook her head, trying to free her mind from the hypnotizing effect of the voice, not sure exactly what had happened. The creatures silently eyed her and waited. She knew they were no danger to her.

She removed the sniper rifle from her back and lay down on the sand in the shooter's prone position. She put her eye to the sight. Out of the corner of her eye she saw the creatures retreat slightly as if they were afraid to be too close to this act of ecstatic violence, afraid that it would be too powerful to be seen without bringing death to the voyeur as well.

Macaria stared through the scope as the strange storm reached the trio. They were hidden by the maelstrom for about thirty seconds; then the storm passed over them and disappeared back into the gray ash, blowing out long before it reached her position. The woman, Alma, was kneeling in the sand and crying. Alex was holding her.

Blake was on shaky legs holding his head. She had no idea what had happened to them and wasn't interesting in finding out for herself.

A strange figure emerged from the Veil, its body misshapen, appendages appearing from the wrong places. An arm jutted from the right hip, while other parts of its body seemed unformed, as if it had not been fully baked when removed from the oven. It took a few steps but then stood in wait.

Blake helped Alma up and gave her a hug, and they all began to move towards the strange figure. Now is the time, she thought.

She would kill this trio. She would go past the Veil and kill whatever was there. Then she would make her way to the tower, kill its inhabitant, and destroy the pivot of the world. She was going to strike at the axis mundi, the sacred mountain, the heart of the Strands of the universe. Her job was extinction—blessed death.

This was not about killing a person, or about killing humankind. It was about killing the universe, ending its dreadful tyranny. For this world was insane. With every breath it bred crazy. It had had its chance and the only thing that would fix it was to start back at zero.

She set the crosshairs on Blake's back, calculated drop and wind, corrected, and squeezed the trigger. There was a deafening crack as the bullet flew from the barrel, lead death ready to change the world. This trumpet of violence was not dulled or swallowed up by the dead air but magnified with each echoed revolution until it was the volume of a sonic boom. The bullet streaked towards its target creating circular ripples that scarred the soupy gray mist and expanded outward.

As she watched the trajectory a growing sense of unease developed in her gut. She knew that something was wrong, something bad was about to happen. She could feel it in every black part of her. But all she could do at that instant was watch.

CHAPTER 12

Blake was staring at the Veil when he felt a drop in pressure. His ears popped and he saw something rising from the desert floor in front of the Veil. It looked like a gathering of shadows coalescing, single dark Strands weaving in and out of each other.

"What is that?" Alma asks nervously.

"Nothing good." Blake looked to Alex for answers. "Should we run?"

"Don't bother, it will be quick. We couldn't outrun it anyway."

Blake didn't have time to ask another question. The tendrils swirled, approaching them quickly, like a dark wall of squirming eels. As they got closer Blake saw images forming in the web. They were the nightmares and dark memories of the Strands, the dark shadows behind the dreams of greatness, love, and happiness.

The storm hit him like a pounding wave, pushing him back, as it ripped through his mind. Images flashed like a strobe through his awareness: A dead man with puke on his face and a needle in his arm—much like his friend Martin has looked when he died. A child hit by a car, the drunk driver running over her as she chases a ball into the road. A woman screaming for help as two men hold her down and hit her repeatedly with a brick. He didn't see complete stories, but when the images flashed through him he instantaneously knew their history and their future.

The pain of these images and memories tore through his body. He felt the pounding of the brick, experienced the last painful thoughts of the junkie. It hurt parts of him he didn't even know were there, parts of him that he'd hidden from the world so that they couldn't be exposed and filleted and dissected. What had Martin thought of as he died? What had Blake's mother thought? But there would be no answers here, no epiphanies.

The pain seemed to go on and on, looping back on him again and again. He faintly heard crying in the distance. He didn't want to see or feel any more.

"Stop it," he whispered. His mind began to shatter. He was losing. He couldn't get out. The darkness was claiming him.

He slowly realized that the sounds of weeping came from Alma. He focused on her sobbing, trying to bring himself back. "Stop it!" he shouted.

Her cries became louder, more insistent. He heard Alex telling her, "It's going to be all right, it's over now." The images slowed, the pain releasing as the dark tendrils pulled back from his mind, their icy fingers receding.

"STOP!" he bellowed.

He was back. His vision cleared from black to gray and then he was staring at Alex, who was holding Alma. She was on her knees, crying. He didn't need to ask why. Behind him the dark cloud returned to the sand, disappearing as quickly as it had appeared.

Alma stares at him, "That was fucking awful."

"I know."

"That is only the second time I've encountered that in the Strands." Alex adds.

"What was it?"

"I don't know. But my theory is that it's the Strands' way of trying to illuminate the darkness. Remember how I said that all systems have methods of self-correcting? I think that dark storm is one method. What it does, why it appears when it does, I don't know."

Alex turned back to the Veil. "Daath has arrived."

Blake followed Alex's gaze to see a figure emerging from the Veil. The figure was disfigured, with limbs in the wrong places. Parts of its skin and anatomy did not look completely formed. Liquid epithelial tissue and twisting features searched for the correct configuration. It wore a cloak with a dark hood that hid its face in shadow. It was naked otherwise, but due to its shifting anatomy it was impossible for him to tell whether it was male or female, if those concepts even applied here.

"Daath?" Blake asked.

"Yes. It will bring you through the Veil to Damcar."

Blake began to walk towards Daath. He'd only taken two steps when there was the loud crack of thunder reverberating through the air. Blake turned and suddenly Alma was falling lifelessly towards him.

Silence. He caught her body as it fell. She was already dead, eyes staring into the abyss, blood streaming from the exit wound in her chest. No time for him to say he was sorry, to say he loved her, to say anything.

Anger rose in him, burning through his insides as he looked down at her lifeless brown eyes. Those eyes. The only eyes in all of creation that seemed to look through him to the man he could be. They were eyes that saw the world for what it could be, not just what it was. Now they searched nothing; that penetrating intelligence and love was gone.

When the anger rose to his throat, he let loose a primordial scream that was both beautiful and terrifying. It was a scream capable of bringing new worlds into existence, or ending them.

He let her small body spill to the ground as he stood. On the crest of the hill stood the death-bringer. He could feel her black energy emanating in waves and ripples through the air. Here was a singularity, a black hole in the Strands. Her power ripped through the air and galvanized his skin. She was a force of the Strands, a physical principle of the system, one of its principal players forcing the rest of the pawns to move.

He could sense not only her devotion to death but her yearning to understand it. What is its meaning? Where does it lead? And for all her darkness there was one pinprick of light he could sense. He fumbled toward it with his mind.

Without knowing what he was doing, he began to swing his arm and twirl his hand. He didn't know whether he was doing it correctly. At this moment, he was a vessel for some force. He allowed himself to believe for an instant that Alma's disembodied consciousness had found a way to enter him and direct his actions so that he could make this right. He hoped that was true.

Time slowed, dripped, stopped, and then quickly ran in reverse, moving back far enough for him to make a difference. Again he was watching Daath walk through the Veil, but this time he knew what was about to occur. Quickly, he told himself. Again he circled his arm, the portal forming between his fingers, then expanding.

"Get down!" he yelled.

No one questioned. Alex and Alma fell to the ground.

He was facing the bullet. It made ripples through the air, concentric circles expanding outward, as if the bullet were a lead pebble cast into a still lake, its violence sending shock waves through the Strands. Reaching into the mind of the killer atop the dune, he pulled at that pinprick of light she had tried to hide, the only dimension where she felt love, and expanded it. He connected that reality with the bullet and the lead death it promised.

As he expanded the portal, the killer screamed—and so did Alex.

"Blake, no!" Alex yelled. "Collapse it. Collapse it now!"

Time was moving extremely slow. Blake moved to the left of the portal and looked in. An older man was standing in front of a window looking out at a city. He was holding a glass tumbler, golden brown liquid swirling at the bottom. Then the man turned and stared directly at him, and the woman behind him. He raised his glass as if toasting the apocalypse, took a sip—

The world lurched back to normal speed, the scene jumping forward as if a grinding gear had finally caught. The glass shattered and a dark hole appeared in the man's forehead. He fell backward silently. The portal winked shut.

The murderer shrieked and began running down the dune towards them. Blake heard an eruption of sound, metal clashing against metal, as a sea of crimson creatures swarmed over the top of the dune to follow their goddess into battle. Blake could only stand and stare at the spectacle as a sea of blood-red alien crabs, washed down towards them, the screeching metal a preamble to a crash.

"Blake, do something." It was Alma, alive again—but for how long? Had he reshaped her destiny? The Strands now struggling to put things back the way they should be and take her life?

His fingers itched, the feeling rising up his arms like an electric shock. "All right, let's try again."

He thought time would run in reverse again, but no portal formed between his hands. Instead a black cloud rose from the sand. The hungry eels of the Strand storm emerged from the desert floor, searching for prey, searching for a way to unburden themselves of the darkness they carried. The storm whipped across this wasteland slamming into their attacker and the crabs. The woman was screaming, as the eels intensified her darkness, ripping apart her mind. The crabs crashed against the dark wall like a wave against a jetty, the first dozen rows sent careening backward.

When Blake had been in the storm, it had felt like the torture would never end, but for the observer it only lasted a few seconds. The cloud moved past her and then receded back below the sands of the dune.

What happens now? he wondered. Have the Strands self-corrected or is she going to turn around and kill us? Would that be self-correcting?

The woman turned to face them. She raised her arms. "Death to death," she whispered.

The crabs swarmed, their teeth a cacophonous requiem. She did not scream as the crabs unmade her, washing over her like a tidal wave. When the wave receded there was a red phantom form, arms outstretched, a cloud of pink clinging to the shape of life as if she could be stitched back together from the blood particles that remained—and then it was gone. He wondered what she had seen, what the dark storm had shown her.

"What have you done, Blake?" There were tears in Alex's eyes. "You killed Romero."

Alma stood up. "What the fuck are you talking about? I didn't see Blake shoot anyone. She was the one with the gun."

"But he joined two dimensions so that the bullet would hit him."

"I wouldn't have known how to do that even if I wanted to." Blake realized that they did not remember the alternate Strand in which Alma died by that same bullet. He wanted to keep that secret; it would be hard on Alma. "I felt... directed." He didn't add that his theory was that he had become possessed by the spirit of Alma.

Alex sat back glumly. "Romero was my best friend. I always hoped he'd leave Strand Corporation the way I had. I sometime feel like he stayed to protect Macaria, although she would have left if he'd asked her to. I don't know why he stayed. I guess he felt he was doing the right thing. At the end when he realized what was happening he raised that glass and looked at me as if to say, 'Cheers, this is as good an end as any, thanks for the ride.' He seemed resigned, almost relieved."

"That was Macaria, the Shadow?"

"Yes. Romero was the only father she ever had and her bullet killed him. He'd ordered her to kill hundreds of people and in the end he was killed by her. Poetic."

"Does someone need passage through the Veil?" The voice was deep and resonant. They had forgotten about Daath. It had continued to approach them as they conversed.

No one spoke, and Daath did not seem to command a response. It appeared willing to wait silently. Blake still couldn't see its face. He turned from the wondrous creature, still feeling that odd sense that something was not quite right, that turning from such miracles seemed far too easy and commonplace, as if all this was a dream that he would wake from. His mind seemed to be accepting this all too easily.

He turned back to Alex. "Alex, come with us now. There is nothing more to do now that Romero and Macaria are gone."

"I have to go back. Strand Corporation does not die with Romero or the Shadows. Strangely enough, they were fighting to keep it more grounded in spirituality, wanting to arrest its slide towards a purely capitalist machine. I think... seeing Romero die, I realized what a friend he was. He just lost his way somehow, and that could happen to any of us." Alex shook his head. "I want to shake Strand Corporation to the ground so that no one else has to die because of a list, so that people don't go on believing that the capitalist consumer reality is the only way." He took a moment to breathe. "Besides, you don't need me. From here on in it's all new."

Alex extended his hands towards Blake. Blake took them. "Good luck, Alex."

"Thanks for your help," Alma said. She gave Alex a hug.

"Good luck to both of you. I don't know if we'll ever see each other again, but I was glad to have known you for the time I did. I look forward to the next chapter or verse. It's the life of an inch. I hope to see you on the other side of it." Alex smiled, waved his arms, and was pulled into the vortex. Gone.

They both stood and looked at Daath. Blake took Alma's hand and squeezed.

"We're ready now."

"Your tokens, please?"

"Tokens?" Blake and Alma exchanged glances, not sure whether Alex had forgotten a piece of vital information before leaving them.

"You must give me something you cherish to cross."

"Why?" Alma asks of the faceless form.

"It has always been. I know not why."

Blake knew there was only one thing to give. He reached into his pocket and took out the silver medallion that his mother had given him. He looked at the face one last time, the familiar scene of Saint David of Wales preaching from a raised mound, a dove on his shoulder. To finding answers, mom. He kissed it and handed it to Daath. It sank into the skin of its hand and disappeared.

Alma stepped forward and removed the cross from her neck. There was a tear in her eye. He knew what this meant to her. It was like giving away that memory of her father, like resigning it to the hall of forgotten memories. She placed the cross and the chain in Daath's hand and it too was absorbed.

"You must hold onto my cloak as we go through the Veil. Hold tight and do not let go. To get lost in the Veil is to be lost in limbo for eternity."

They walked towards the Veil. Its surface became more active, bubbling like a cauldron waiting for the main ingredient in the witch's brew: two fattened souls. Blake shivered.

"Anything else we need to know?" Alma asked as she clutched more tightly at Daath's cape, her knuckles white.

"You will each experience one of your most evolutionary memories."

Blake opened his mouth to ask what that meant, but Daath's body disappeared into the Veil, the undulations of the mercurial wall growing more violent. Blake had a moment to contemplate letting go, but then he saw Alma enter and knew he must go through with her. He held tight, the silver liquid reflecting his fear back at him as he stepped into himself and his worst nightmare.

CHapTer 13

He was not surprised by the images that rose before him. He could think of no other memory that had been more integral to his development. This was the nightmare he expected to see, the one that had plagued him most of his life. Would this be the last time he would have to relive the event? Was the aim of showing it this one last time to allow him to move past it?

As always, he was viewing the events through his 12-year-old eyes—doomed, to relive the whole thing, not just the sights and sounds, but the feelings, the experience. He was like an omniscient narrator in his own memory, his own body, with the 12-year-old and 30-year-old selves sharing headspace for this singular purpose.

Even now he could feel the elation when he opened the door to the kitchen and shrugged out of his backpack. It was filled with homework and books, the last remaining albatross of a day at school. It had been a day of drudgery and complete boredom with spoon-fed book learning. His teachers had had their own dreams crushed to oblivion and couldn't wait to do the same to their students.

But that was done for now, and releasing himself from the crushing weight of the books and the sentiment that went with them made him feel that much lighter, happier, as if true joy could only be felt after comparative suffering. The book bag fell to the floor and school was forgotten.

When he opened the door to the refrigerator, claiming his Holy Coke, he felt something amiss. His mother was not sitting in her usual spot at the kitchen table.

"Mom," he called. He listened for any sounds in the house and heard none. It was odd but not something that scared him. Not something that demanded his immediate attention the way the sugary sweetness in his hand did. He popped the top on the Coke can and took a quick sip as foam began to rise.

"Ahhh": a satisfied sigh.

Yes, he'd always remember that. How good that soda tasted. It emptied his mind of concern. He drank it slowly, wanting to relish the taste. It was most definitely the best drink he'd ever had, would ever have. His mother lay dead or dying just a few doors down and yet here he was enjoying a soda. Guilt was the most prominent feeling for his observing older self, but he also felt the stirrings of cruel destiny. For if he had questioned his mother's absence, had seen something ominous in it, maybe he could have saved her. But also if he'd gone through his normal routine, taken a quick sip, and then gone to the bathroom like he'd done every other day, maybe he could have helped or at least held her hand as she passed.

Why? Why of all days did he choose today to break from ritual? Why did the goddamn soda taste so good, so much better than any other time? Why?

He wiped his mouth and slammed the can down on the counter, mimicking movies where cowboys slammed their empty shot glasses down on the bar and then quickly went for their guns, violently satisfied. The Coke ran through his system quickly and now he felt the overwhelming need to relieve his bladder.

He ran down the hall, unzipping his jeans on the way. When he entered the bathroom he didn't even bother to close the door behind him. He had eyes only for the toilet. As he began to relieve himself he was surprised at how white the world seemed. Sunlight was shining through the high window over the tub to his left, the white tile, sink, toilet, gleaming in its light.

The tub. The tub. Calling his vision to its dark revelation. His piss stopped in midstream and at first he felt only embarrassment as he saw his mother's hand lying over the tub edge, palm up. He followed it to her naked breasts, her pale, beautiful face, her dark hair floating around her, a shadowy halo.

Red-faced, he quickly zipped up. He'd never felt so ashamed before.

"Mom, I'm sorry... I... I was just..." he stammered, believing he'd caught her unaware and hoping to God that she'd not seen his penis.

But there was an oddity to this scene. An oddity that became all too apparent as his shame began to ebb and the red truth was revealed.

Red. That was what had pulled at the corners of his vision: a line of red that ran from a small pool on the tile at the side of the tub to his mother's wrist. And once seeing it, it became his world. Red everywhere. The tub filled with it, her arm a red river, opened from wrist to elbow; a red sea of death parting her flesh. It eclipsed his vision, following his screams down this red tunnel of madness as he passed out.

As 12-year-old Blake lay unconscious, his 30-year-old self pondered the ways this terrible experience had shaped him. It was her death that had pushed him towards the occult and philosophy. He'd wanted to find meaning in death, but also he wanted to fend off whatever insanity or soul-sickness was capable of driving someone to an act of suicide. He felt that dark shadow in his personality, the incessant pessimism that tilted him toward depression. There were no silver linings to his dark clouds; there was only rain. His mother had been a writer, a poet, as he had become, and he felt his whole life was spinning in that direction. He was a psychology major in college and the occult seemed a perfect marriage with it. The occult was practical psychology, in his opinion: a means of changing thought patterns, creativity, mental outlook. It was designed to hook into the spiritual and guide the mind to new heights.

For a time it had done exactly that. But somewhere along the way he lost his passion for it. He questioned whether becoming a writer was a good idea, especially a writer of occult experiences and fiction; once it became a profession, it lost some of its luster. His passion began to waver and he again found himself asking what his purpose was, for it didn't seem like he'd found it.

Then his friend Martin committed suicide. Martin was an artist like him, a painter, one of his best friends. From the outside looking in, one would say Martin was successful, he lived his dream, he had everything he'd ever wanted—success, money, fame— but in the end he found those things hadn't given him peace or happiness. Blake knew what it was like to compare his reality with what he saw in others' lives; he found himself wanting more, though their gleaming facades were seemingly unachievable. Everyone seemed successful and content, but him. He found that once he got everything he thought he wanted, it either wasn't what he expected or not what he really wanted at all. And where did one go from there? For Martin, the only answer was death.

Blake had begun to feel the same. And that fear that he so dreaded in the wake of his mother's death returned, the fear that this fate was his as well, that one day he just wouldn't be able to take it anymore and would find that fighting it was useless. Just give in. Give in to death and the gift of absence it offered.

The haze cleared and he was looking at his mother's hand, a bead of blood falling from her index finger and joining the rest of her blood that pooled on the tile. That was what he continued to stare at once he awoke from passing out. He lay there for hours, in shock, until his father finally came home and found him on the bathroom floor. There was screaming, crying, disbelief, pain beyond pain. The lives they had lived were over; what came after would never be the same.

The curtain of memory began to draw aside, replaced by a smoky mist—Daath's cloak. Then Damcar was before him and it was nothing like what he had expected.

CHapTer 14

Alma was not surprised by her memory either. This was the incident that had introduced her to Blake, the sour taste of revelation, and the gratitude of being alive. It also was the culmination of a long journey in which she had traveled the world in search of the universal Beat. After her eighteenth birthday, she had said her goodbyes to her family and told them that she was beginning a pilgrimage in which she would learn all she could of music, the occult, and art. She wanted to be a singer, songwriter, and guitarist; more than that, she wanted to invent a new form of music that would encompass the spiritual, occult, and alchemical principles of transformation and transmutation while embodying the musical styles and sound of all the world's religious and occult traditions and cultures.

What she was really after, whether she had known it or not, was creating a new form of magic. All things vibrated at a certain frequency, and her subtle control of those tones and frequencies could bring about changes in neural chemistry that led to altered states of consciousness.

It had begun as a quest to gather the music of the world and collect it, spice it up, transform it; like a modern-day Grimm, except that Alma was trafficking in beat and rhythm instead of stories and lore. She collected rhythms and riffs like charms. Each had a pulse that breathed in new life.

In the desert canyons of Arizona she had seen something that altered the nature of this quest. The Hopi of Black Mesa had invited her to participate in one of their rituals, the goal of which was to enable the shaman to cross over into the Shadow World, where the soul of their beat had been formed. As she ingested the magic buttons, the manna of the desert, the cadence had begun. Slow... so slow. The pulse of the universe as measured in millennia, only heard in silence and stillness, the slow turn of the world swirling in her brain. Over the course of hours the tempo changed, the shift almost imperceptible unless you were dialed into its hum, its quiet frequency. It was her heart, her head, her blood. The rhythm of her body, the rhythm of her mind became that of the world; the dance of the universe. She—the Earth. The Earth—her. And in that moment she knew it was her mission to find a way to bring that feeling of miraculous unity to others.

The beat arose from her openness to the teachings of gurus, shaman, and priests. They exposed the secrets of their art to her and from this arose the beat, the heart. This was what she collected, adding each new beat to the one before. What had at first sounded like a cacophony developed into a symphony of the soul. She had become the tonal alchemist, and her Great Work was the transformation of sound into ecstatic enlightenment.

Plucking at the strings of revelation and pounding on the skin of its drums, Alma listened intently to the rhythm she was creating until there was but one beat left to find. Behind each note there was an emptiness that she could feel more than hear, a harmonic vacuum that needed to be filled in order for the Great Work to be complete. The search for that final tone had brought her to Peru, feeling a terror so deep she didn't know it was possible to be so frightened and yet still be alive.

Alive... was she? She'd been alone in the jungle for how long? Hours? Days? She couldn't remember. Even her body seemed unable to tell time. When was the last time she'd eaten? Pissed? Shit? Slept? Perhaps she had died and entered a world between worlds, a wasteland where fear and doubt were the only emotions.

Mouth dry, throat lined with dirt, Alma sat and waited in the stillness of expectant epiphany. She was dehydrated, and each time she attempted to swallow it felt like razorblades were slicing her esophagus. Her stomach rumbled, a sound born of the hunger and the raw fear that clawed at her insides. Each time the search was the same but different. Was she closer now? It was so hard to tell on a journey such as this. A quest of the spirit had no landmarks.

The Ancient Ones, descendants of the shamans of Machu Picchu, who some believed had been aliens from an alternate spiritual dimension, had given Alma the sacred stone to ingest. It set her blood to boiling, her brain afire, dendritic roots ablaze in a pool of incendiary hallucinogenic tribal drug. Fear seeped into her, the roots of the massive trees becoming those of her neurons, dripping poison into the black abyss of her synapses. The world was an ocean of fear, emanating from her fevered brain, then out to the black rotting earth, and back again; crashing upon her in scorching waves that tore through her skin, peeling back the mask of skin, burning through her muscles to expose the raw nerve below. Tongues dripping with acid licked at her very core until the pain and fear obliterated all else and there was no Alma. No her. No inside and no outside. She was All and All was terror.

When she thought she could take no more, when she truly believed she had died, IT appeared, standing silently within the massive roots of the ancient trees, seemingly part of them, birthed from the rough bark, expelled as a disease; the dual god of light and dark, life and death, pain and ecstasy. ITs skin was the color of ash. Long dirty ropes of hair framed the horrid face in a weave of darkness, twisted like the roots that covered every inch of the forest, shadowing ITs features and then pulling back as if to fully reveal the face beneath. Black slits for eyes, the lids sewn shut with rough stitching the consistency of bark. Mouth shut by the same demonic surgeon. IT was a mute archangel, the patchwork of ITs flesh making IT look like a rag doll spit from the pit of madness.

Alma's heart seemed ready to explode. The pulse in her veins was that of the jungle. The thing made no move, but ITs mere presence was that of death. IT was the Devil, the Ancient One come to obliterate the world.

Alma turned and ran. She did not need to look behind her to know that IT followed. She could hear ITs footfalls stalking her. ITs contact with the earth sent tremors through the roots, delivering a black pulse through Alma's body that she was incapable of resisting. ITs rhythm became hers, impossible to break. At that moment she felt the beat. And it was terrible. It was darkness. It was fear. It was all things wrong with the world. It was Death. It was her. The end of all things. The death of the life she knew.

Something deep inside her knew that beyond the chasm, beyond the overwhelming fear was a world of light, a world of freedom. If she could only give up her fear and let herself fall through the darkness it would all be over. The light would be All. She would be Home, the place where the beat never needed to change because it was perfect.

But she couldn't. Couldn't stop running. Couldn't turn to face the demon that gave chase. She shivered in the drowning humidity, her lungs afire, acid burning through her muscles. She was going to die. The moment she stopped the demon would have her and tear this worthless costume of flesh to pieces.

She couldn't last much longer. Waves of fire danced before her eyes. The jungle pulsed red, the forest floor a tapestry of roots that threatened to twist an ankle or ensnare a foot at every stride. The roots throbbed, the veins of a much larger body, the macrocosm to her microcosm. If she could but find its powerful heart maybe that would protect her. But where would the heart of such a being reside. How far away? In what deep hidden cave would the heart of Gaia live?

She began to scream. A primordial, blood-curdling scream, like that which had brought the world into existence. Her feet stumbled, the life force in them finally giving way to the demands and laws of the physical universe. By pure will she was able to keep her feet beneath her but she knew she would not last much longer. What hope did she have of outrunning this beast? But even without hope she would not give in because the fear of what chased her was so complete that she would struggle and fight to keep IT away even if it was only for another moment.

Alma had traveled many planes of existence and she recognized this one for what it was: Hell. The Lord of Illusions, the ultimate evil, was pulling at her, willing her to accept the only fate she would ever know.

Death.

"NOOOOOO—"

A light shone through the pulsing black and red of the forest. It was merely a pinprick at first, but as she ran towards it, its power and warmth grew with each step.

"Save me," she prayed. "Please save me."

A being stepped from behind the shadow of a tree, its hair dancing fire, skin glittering gold and then burning to white, blazing like a sun: a god of light, the antithesis to the dark lord that chased her.

"Save me," she whispered more to herself than to the deity. For what deity needed to hear the cries of its creations? It knew her heart, knew of her desire to escape the demon that hunted her, knew of her unabashed desire to live, no matter how illusory or tenuous that existence was.

The god took a step forward and reached to its side to tear a round orb from its hip. It brought the orb to its mouth and spit fire into it until it burned an angry crimson, like the jungle—like the demon. The deity hurled the flaming sphere in a series of fluid motions that held more likeness to dance than combat.

The comet flew past Alma and she could feel the projectile's heat as it passed her face. Turning, she followed its trajectory to the demon that was closing in on her. The world behind was darkness and fear. Immediately the terror pulled at her heart as she saw her pursuer only a few feet away.

The ball of light hit the demon in the forehead. The stitches of ITs mouth stretched in an inaudible scream, as light filled IT. Like a balloon, IT expanded with light till ITs dark, tattered flesh could no longer contain it, exploding outward, leaving behind only the orb, the seed of light.

Alma, shaking, almost as scared of her savior as she had been of the demon, turned. A god that wielded such power could just as easily blast her from existence.

The luminous being pulsed once, twice, and slowly color began to bleed back into the world, covering this new messiah in the fleshy mask of humanity. The blazing light was now little more than a glimmer. But when he approached Alma she could still see the god in his eyes, the demiurge, the fire of creation, the Spirit of All.

The angel extended his arm, holding an open hand out to Alma.

"My name is Blake. Can you walk?"

Alma nodded, incapable of speech, awed by her savior's presence.

"Then walk with me."

***

Soon after this event she had started her band, and this experience had led to the name Dark-Revelations. Every song, every rhythm, contained that dark pulse that wove through the song—sometimes prominent, sometimes notable by its absence, but always there. It was the tick of time, the beat of death, the end of existence. That last beat was what kept us all driven to succeed, to push on, to find answers. And without it, our lives, like the song, were meaningless.

She never asked Blake what he had experienced that day. She didn't want to taint the magic of it and she had asked him never to reveal it either in conversation or in his books. She had told her version of it in song, but what he saw, what he experienced, was still a mystery to her. What she knew, what would never change, was the knowledge that Blake had saved her that day. Whether the demon was literal or a metaphorical manifestation of her psyche didn't matter. What mattered is that she would have been lost to the darkness if that demon had caught her. She would have been lost to the darkness of the world, the darkness within herself.

The darkness gave way to haze and she blinked, staring at the black cloak of Daath. Blake was to her left. She then looked over Daath's shoulder and whispered to herself, "Not exactly what I thought Heaven would look like."

CHAPTER 15

At first Blake only saw the small pueblo-like buildings made of hardened sand, or perhaps they were caves created by digging into the hardpan of a butte. It hardly seemed like a place from which enlightenment might be attained. As he let go of the cape, Daath stepped to one side and Blake gasped.

The dwellings were squat so that they would not interrupt the expanse. Surrounding them in a large ellipse were the Strands. They looked like tentacles swimming and coiling in intertwined glass tubes that formed a wall around the village of Damcar. It was not a large area, but a cozy pocket from which one could observe the innumerable marvels of the world.

At the far end of the ellipse, the tubes of the Strands came to a single point and then streamed into the Tower. The structure itself was beautiful. It looked perfectly smooth, its dark glass surface partially reflecting the Strands that entered it; its base glowed with multicolored splendor and the archway of the gate looked like a rainbow. Further up, the colors faded like a sunset etched in dark stone. This then gave way to the amber glow of an absent sun. For all Blake knew, the Tower was the source of that candle-flame glow as it was the source of the Strands.

Higher still and there was the balcony and its dark occupant. Now he could see its dark robes, its hooded face, and a flash of eyes that looked out upon Damcar and the Strands from its regal perch.

"You can feel it, like a vibration. In my head it brings out colors and music." Alma was staring off at the Tower. Her eyes were bright, and her mouth hung open in wonderment.

Blake had been concentrating on what he could see. Now he closed his eyes, realizing that sight was interfering with his other senses; there was just too much newness to examine. When he closed his eyes he could feel it. It was a pleasant vibration, a hum. Alma was right: it was like music singing in his bones, in his heart, expanding in his mind and throughout his whole body, making him feel like he was intimately tied into the whole thing, the Strands, the Tower, Damcar, himself. All one. All intimately intertwined, the fate of one, the fate of all. The beauty of one, the beauty of all.

"Yes," he whispered. "I feel it."

He opened his eyes. His senses married and he was able to take in the scene, not just with his eyes but with his whole being. This place was magic. It was miracle. And he understood why some of the people Alex had led here may have decided to spend lifetimes in its presence.

On the heels of that thought he wondered what walking into the Tower would feel like, the very origin and nexus of these miracles. Of all those that had come to Damcar, how many had entered the

Tower? For as near as he was, this was an observation point. Close but separate.

From one of the caves in the butte directly opposite him, a human form emerged, wrapped in dark robes. For the moment its face was indistinct, hidden in the shadow of the hood it wore, but Blake knew it was not human. Its bare feet and hands contained longer digits and its skin seemed woven of the same mercurial substance that made the Veil. When it pulled back the cowl, revealing its silver features, dark eyes stared back at him, reflecting a warped image of Blake's face. For a moment those black eyes only reflected, but as he stared deeper, a fire storm started working its way out from the center, until a tempest of colors swarmed throughout the theatre of its eyes. It was the Strands swirling there, replayed in the creature's vision, the movie of the universe captured and replayed over and over. The creature blinked and the storm ended replaced by deep black pools.

"Hello. My name is Seriph one of the Geburiak. Welcome to Damcar." Its voice was deep like that of the Daath's, but it also contained an echo delay; the first syllable of a word was still resonating as the second syllable was sounded.

"Blake," Blake said. He extended his hand out of habit.

Seriph's features swam, becoming almost human momentarily, and then coalesced back into its alien form. It grasped Blake's hand. When their flesh came in contact it was as if the hand formed as they shook, taking that form only as it became necessary. It felt like shaking a hand made of Jell-O.

"Alma." Alma stepped forward and offered her hand, which Seriph took. She grimaced slightly as Seriph's hand molded around hers, as if she'd just touched something slimy and unformed.

Seriph stepped back, its features continuing to swim, its eyes going from mirror black to swirling colors and back again. The storm of its face made Blake dizzy. Seriph seemed to recognize this and replaced the cowl, again shading its face in shadow. It did not speak but stood waiting.

There were so many questions running through Blake's mind about Damcar, the Tower, the Strands, Guburiak, that he stood there slack jawed his lips trying to form a question that wouldn't come.

"So Damcar. What the fuck is it?" Alma said. Blake felt a rush of affection for her: always defiant, even in the midst of wonders.

"It is a holy instant. It sits between the Nexus and the Veil and was created when the Strands left the Tower and then separated, expanding outward. It is the abyss between primal consciousness and ego consciousness, leading to illuminated consciousness."

Alma pointed at the Tower. "And that is illuminated consciousness."

"No," Seriph said, shaking its hooded head. "That is still ego consciousness. It exists in a plane that can still be perceived by the senses and by the mind. Its lessons still act in the realm of spiritual revelation. Illuminated consciousness and true knowledge can only be found beyond the Tower."

"And what is beyond the Tower?" Blake asked.

"There are many names for it: The Ain, Nothing, Heaven, Universal consciousness, God. But words fail as do human conceptions once one goes beyond the Tower, because nothing in this world makes sense beyond the Tower. Not your thoughts, your egos, your bodies. It is a world beyond your ability to conceive."

Blake looked to the Nexus, where all the Strands seemed to run into each other: millions of strings looking like aggravated snakes fighting to get into the Tower, while others fought to get out.

"Are the Strands coming from the Tower or going into it?"

"Both. Neither. Whatever may appear, the Strands do not have the same conception of time. You can enter a Strand at one point or another. From Damcar I could enter a single Strand in the future and then go to what other beings in that Strand would perceive as the past. I could witness the death of someone who'd not yet been born. I could prophesize the exact moment of his death and to all those who heard me it would seem as if I was a god."

"But you don't do that?" asked Alma.

"Some of us have. But it is frowned upon. It is our way of amusing ourselves. Maybe it doesn't seem funny to those outside, but for us change is slow. Damcar is not part of the Strands, and although we exist in the system of the Tower, time as such moves extremely slowly or is at least perceived by us that way. Many of us have experienced millions of lifetimes from this very spot."

Blake looked around and gaped. Hundreds of forms, all similar to Seriph, now stood around them, forming a wide circle.

"What are you? Why are you here?"

"We are historians of a sort," Seriph said, "collecting the experiences of the Strands—for what purpose we are not sure. Like Daath we have given up what we once were when we began to travel within the multiverse of the Strands. Our bodies and minds changed in order to accommodate existence in multiple dimensions simultaneously and through the years our histories became part of the collective shared consciousness of the tribe of Geburiak. Our personal experience no longer had meaning. Sometimes we use our collected knowledge to help seekers like you and to explain as best we can the structure of the Strands and the Tower. At other times we just exist in the happiness of this eternal moment."

"And what would be the point of entering the Tower?" Alma asked.

"Only the person who looks to enter the Tower can answer that question."

"But there have been others who've told you of their motivations."

"True enough. Some believe it is to find God. Others to know the truth. Still others who can't dismiss their pure curiosity and just need to know what is in there. The most popular reason is that knowledge ends at the Veil, and from here only experience will result in epiphany. At the Veil you gave up a part of yourself; then you were reminded of another part of yourself, that part of yourself that seeks answers. From Damcar you can see that the knowledge contained in the Strands will not explain to you or allow you to understand why they exist. In crossing the Veil you moved from a world that could be explained by thinking about it, learning about it, into a world that will only make sense through experience. It can only make sense with spirit logic, not head logic."

Blake thought about that, aware of the irony. True, he had learned many things in the Strand of his life but it did not allow him to break out of that rut and learn what he so desperately wanted to know: Why was he here? What was his true purpose? Was there more? What he stared at now showed that there was indeed more. A lot more. And what would the Tower show him?

But Alma had one more question. "Who built all this?"

"You, Alma. Everyone. Everyone who creates. Everyone with the courage to make choices creates a Strand."

"I understand that. What I meant, was who started it? Who or What said, 'Let there be light'?"

"Ahh, yes, the age-old question. The question that is always asked."

Blake waited breathlessly as Seriph seemed to weigh how it was going to begin.

"We do not know."

Blake let out a sigh. Nothing new here. The same old half-answers that looped back on themselves to yet more questions.

"That is a question only you can answer. It is a question that is based on your belief in your own purpose. The purpose of the Strands: are they reality or a spiritual tool, or a playground. Are they meant to show you the impossibility of separation, the importance of awakening to your higher self, or was it once a utopia that has run down and needs to be fixed or obliterated and restarted? Was it Macaria who was meant to breach the Veil and not you? For she would have come here to destroy it. Which leads to so many more interesting questions. Could she have? Would we have let her? If there was a god, would he or she or they or it have let her?" Seriph shrugged. "Or is this all just a grand game that you forgot you were playing, forgetting the rules and objectives, trying to get back to the beginning so you can remind yourself it was all just a dream? All good questions and theories. All ones we have heard before. But as Geburiak we only watch. We collect, we help where we can, but we can't interpret, surmise, or theorize. That is for those who exist in the system, not here outside of it."

"And what of the person who lives in the Tower?" Blake pointed up to the dark figure who watched them from the balcony.

"Again, we do not know. Maybe that person is the architect of the system. God. Maybe the landlord scrutinizing the show to make sure you all pay the rent or that the heat doesn't go off. Maybe a watcher like us, storing history, or maybe calculating how it will all work out, hoping to fix it or condemn it. Maybe an engineer who keeps it all running, tirelessly making calculations, examining gauges, and turning cogs to keep the lights on, so to speak."

"Sounds like a lot of interpretation, surmising, and theorizing," Alma interjected.

"No. I am merely recounting the ideas expressed by others that have asked similar questions as they stood here as you do now." Seriph paused for a moment. "Do you have any theories or answers you would like me to pass along?"

"No," Blake said. "I have theories but I've grown tired of them. I no longer believe as I once did. I want experience to lead me to belief, and not the other way around."

"That is an answer, Blake. A very important answer. One I will store and recount, for it is unique. And you, Alma?"

"I have only theories for now. To me the Strands are a tool. If what Alex told us is true, then it could take millions of years for a person to experience everything the human body and mind is capable of experiencing before having to repeat. By then we've forgotten we're repeating it. It's like a really, really long movie that it takes years to watch and once it starts over at the beginning again we sort of remember it but then completely forget. The Strands allow us to shorten that time. By entering the Tower we could experience the entire human condition in a moment by experiencing all the

Strands, all the possible quantum states that are capable in this world. It is a spiritual tool that can be used to show us that there is no reason to return, that we have learned everything there is to learn in this form and we can move on."

"I like that very much, Alma. I shall store and recount that as well."

"Now what?"

"You decide. Take your time, for there is plenty of it here."

Blake and Alma walked towards the Nexus to get a better view. The colors swirled and danced before them, a million rainbows streaming in and out of the Tower. Blake was unable to take his eyes from this miracle. It was the first thing he had encountered on this journey that seemed hyper-real, and he could not turn way. This was a phenomenon that commanded his every sense.

"What do you think of all this?" Alma asked, grabbing hold of Blake's hand.

"I'm not sure thinking about it is going to get me anywhere." Blake smiled but it felt wrong on his face, twisted, forced.

"I don't know that I need any more answers," Alma mused. "I think I've seen more than I ever expected and know more than I need. In some cases, ignorance is bliss. All this complexity doesn't mean anything to me."

"But what about the Tower, knowing what's inside, crossing over? What if that is the ultimate aim of our existence? Knowing you are so close, seeing it right in front of you, can you turn away?"

Alma didn't answer.

As they approached the Nexus, the colors of the Strands brightened, the complexity deepening. Each Strand was a separate existence, a universe in a grain of sand. Millions of lives were trapped within those tentacles. The images flowed back and forth, some going out from the direction of the tower, back to the beginning, back to the past, others traveling outward into the future. It was as Alex had said: the quantum phase states of human existence. The totality of human possibilities. If one could step into the single point and experience them all simultaneously then they would experience all it meant to be human and could say goodbye to this tool, this form. For after that what else was there but to repeat it all over again? And that too could be a form of insanity, maybe the most insidious form: doing the same thing over and over again and expecting different results.

Alma stared at the Nexus and its swirling possibilities for a long time.

Finally she said, "Standing here, seeing this miracle so close, realizing that returning to the world of the Strands may be akin to living in an inconsequential loop, I still want to go back. I feel like I've found all I was looking for."

Blake was taken aback. He could not imagine being so close and not wanting to go on. "What do you mean? Found what?"

"I found what I was looking for when you saved me that day. I found hope. I found the beat that I was looking for and I worked it into the rhythm of my life. That's all I ever wanted, to just go with the beat and flow of the music. I wanted to feel like a part of it as its creator and also to make others feel it too. As long as I can do that, I've never had need of anything else. I've seen the bars of my cage and for now I'm happy with them. I don't have the courage to go on. I like being me too much and am afraid that beyond this point I won't be able to be me."

Blake opened his mouth to respond when he felt an enormous pressure in his ears. He whipped around and stared at the Veil. The mist had become a solid mirror—and with a sound like thunder, the mirror began to crack.

CHAPTER 16

Macaria did not understand what had happened at first, why her loyal subjects had turned on her and shredded her until there was nothing left. But then she came to realize that there was no death for death, at least not yet.

She had killed Romero. It hadn't been intentional, but the fact remained that she had fired the bullet that killed the only father she had ever known. With the kind of sardonic irony typical of this twisted universe, Romero had forged the very weapon that killed him. She imagined some hysterical god with bloodshot eyes, staring at a black-and-white television screen that displayed the scene, laughing at the joke it had preordained. That was the system she wanted to destroy. A system that could revel in the pain of others, could take joy in misery, could smirk at death and call it a learning tool. A system such as that could not be repaired; it needed to be leveled to the ground and rebuilt.

At the last she had seen this conviction in Romero's eyes. It was as if the event had been engineered to impart this understanding to him. Seeing the bullet, Macaria, Alex—piecing together the irony that was unfolding—he realized that the system he was struggling to protect was flawed at its base. As he raised his glass, he gave her one of those classic Romero looks, resigned and disgusted at the same time—but at the end there had been the hint of a smile, the corners of his mouth rising uncharacteristically. It also had a suggestion of the sinister, but that was Romero through and through.

She believed that in the end he had seen the wisdom of her words. There was nothing to fear in death. He had fought mortality, had fought cancer, and in the end, death would always come, because it was inevitable. It was built into the system. It was what caused all this pain, and ironically, was the only thing that could save humankind.

She looked to the survivors. Alex had screamed for Blake to close the portal to protect Romero. At the end he had shown his loyalty to Romero, and had realized that although he and Romero had not seen eye to eye on all things, they ultimately had the same goal. Romero had lost his way for a time, and in that sense so had she, but she felt that if Romero had not had a cancerous tumor pushing on his brain and causing him to act from emotion and pain instead of focusing on protecting the miracles of the Strands, things would have been very different. Maybe he and Macaria would have gone rogue as well, and joined forces with Alex. There was no way to know now.

Alex told Blake and Alma what he knew and then sent them on their way, stating that he had to go back. Examining him during this exchange, seeing the sadness in his eyes, she surmised that Romero's death was prompting him to return to the world. He wanted Romero's death to mean something, but he also wanted revenge. She saw the dark shadow that flashed through his eyes, that darkness that longed for violence. When he talked of bringing Strand Corp low she knew that he would enjoy this mission of vengeance. When he was done imparting his knowledge, he handed off the reins to Daath and was gone. There was only one more thing that Blake and Alma could do now—only one direction to go in.

As she followed them towards the Veil, she began to understand why the crabs had blessed her with dismemberment. Approaching the Veil, she could feel an electric current, some galvanizing force that she could sense even as disembodied consciousness. Had she been in her physical form, would it have barred her entry? But what would she do on the other side? Would she be given her body back? It didn't matter; she didn't have a lot of other options. This was her way in.

She did what the others were told and grabbed on to Daath's cloak with mental fingers. She felt pain as they crossed the plane of the Veil and knew with certainty that if she were in her body the Veil would have either expelled her or killed her. Just as the Strand storms were an attempt to expel the darkness of the Strands, the Veil was meant to keep that darkness out of the holy space.

As she entered the Veil she was overwhelmed with the memory of the first time she truly felt the presence of death—not her first kill, but her first after she had become expert, when killing had become automatic, had become art.

***

The shadows enveloped Macaria, hiding her from the prying eyes of her target. She was in her element, invisible unless she chose to make her presence known.

Macaria had been in the closet in the main hallway for hours, waiting patiently for her mark to return. Finally, Benjamin Talos entered the apartment, his keys rattling in the lock. He immediately opened the closet to hang his jacket, damp from a day that had turned from gloomy overcast to drizzling rain.

Muscles coiled, breath held, Macaria pressed herself into deeper shadow, studying the man as he shook rain from his black windbreaker and hung it on a hanger. He placed the hook back on the closet pole only inches from Macaria's face.

There was no hint that the man felt her presence. She felt disappointed. Here was a man who was considered an expert in the occult, one of the few who had learned to be a Conductor on his own, and yet he did not even feel the subtle touch of death. Macaria had not even used her own Conducting powers to hide her presence. In fact, she had a suspicion that Talos would have sensed the pressure created by expanding or collapsing an alternate dimension. Yes, that surely would have been a mistake. The smallest particle of energy delivered from even a small Strand manipulation would have been more than enough for this man to sniff out.

Talos closed the closet door and—ahh, there it was, a twitch of the nose, a whiff of some alien air, a warning rising from the depths of consciousness. A blink. Macaria waited, examining him. She'd seen this dance so many times. The scent of death wafted from her, its potency and immediacy scarring the very air, a warning to those who would listen. She enjoyed this, wondering, almost hoping that just this once she would be surprised and her target would listen to that small yet insistent voice.

With a grunt Talos turned from the closet, dismissing whatever feeling had given him a moment of pause.

Letting the held breath slowly escape her lungs, Macaria allowed her body to relax, cords of wiry muscle unknotting as she prepared to exit and begin the final act of this ballet.

Macaria studied Talos as he made his way down the hallway, wondering what thoughts had crossed through his mind during that instant. Had he smelled death, felt the caress of the winds of fate, heard the voice of God? In all the times she'd seen her targets experience that warning from the universe, not once had she seen one heed its call. And not once had she failed to deliver the death that that intuition was harbinger to. This time would be no exception.

Macaria had found that in the moments before death, when the mark knew it was inevitable, they behaved either far beyond or far below her expectations of them. The emperor became a piece of blubbering flesh begging for his life, while the monk spat with vehemence in her face, daring the bullet. Death had a way of transforming. Regardless of what happened after, its mere shadow had a tendency towards transfiguration. She always wondered what a man would do differently if he knew he had only moments to live. Would he try to escape it or search for some way to meet it head on, accepting the hand of fate, the will of whatever god he prayed to?

Slowly, with feline grace, Macaria slithered from the closet, moving from shadow to shadow down the hall. Talos was sitting at his desk, typing on a keyboard, his eyes riveted to the screen before him, his back to the hallway. Macaria removed the silenced Glock from its holster smoothly and silently. There was still no sign that Talos knew he was going to die.

The room was loud with the hum of his infernal machine. Macaria had an illogical hate for computers. Maybe it was just a symbol of blind modernism, man slowly losing his soul and innate abilities to the humming, insipid, careless machines. Maybe it was that she put more faith in her own abilities and intuitions. But she had to admit that the machine's fans helped to hide the sound of her approach. She was through the room in an instant, the silencer caressing the base of the man's skull like a lover's lips.

To his credit, Talos made no attempt to move. His breath did not even seem to pause or elevate, as if he'd been expecting this all along, and for a moment Macaria wondered whether maybe he had. Had Talos believed the warning? Had he shown Macaria the acceptance she had longed to see? Macaria wanted to ask him whether he had felt death's approach, whether this calm was the evidence of his acceptance. But Macaria had been warned. If she allowed this man to speak she could find the Glock turned on her, and hear herself blessing the bullet that took her life. This man wielded true super-natural power and Macaria respected that.

Macaria paused for a moment, time slowing to a crawl. She tightened her trigger finger ever so slowly, giving the man a moment to do whatever it was he thought important. Talos slowly removed his fingers from the keyboard and placed them on his lap.

"Let this not be the end," he whispered.

Macaria squeezed the trigger and Benjamin Talos's brain splattered over the monitor and wall, a bloody tableau to true knowledge, his last will and testament.

"Let this not be the end" was an adequate prayer, Macaria decided, if that was indeed how Talos had intended it. If this was the end there was not a whole lot of purpose to anything. Yes, a very adequate prayer, she concluded. Maybe the most profound she had heard yet.

Macaria breathed in the silence and time stopped. For the first time she became aware of the holy instant created at the moment of life's annihilation. She basked in this singular moment, the transforming silence. This silence formed a void where death and life battled until that final breath, when the spirit fled the gravitational space of the body, death taking hold of its target, life reclaiming its hold on the survivor. It was a balancing act, and she was able to observe the scale tipping in each direction before settling back into the proper position.

She felt the power in her blood, the raging of her ancestral genes flooding into her cells. Every neuron pulsed in time to a hymn sung in worship to extinction. Standing at the epicenter of this moment, she felt like a goddess, privy to an event only a deity could observe.

It was only a moment, but a moment so complete, prophetic, and revelatory. Macaria instantly acquired an addictive taste for that precious silence, chasing it the way a Buddhist chased nirvana.

The whining of the computer fan shortened the moment, picking at Macaria's attention like nails on a chalkboard. She looked down at the man. Talos appeared to be nothing special in death, but Romero had warned her to be careful. The man wielded power. He was a master of his art. But Macaria was also the master of hers, and it seemed the art of death was more powerful and permanent than that of these spiritual architects who strove to build their heavens.

Macaria removed a thumb drive from her inner coat pocket, shoved it into the computer's USB port, and ran an executable from the command line. The screen went black as the machine's hard drives were wiped.

"Goodbye, Mr. Talos." She bowed in respect. The man had died well, regardless of how he had lived. He had earned this final show of respect.

To be sure there were no traces, Macaria pulled the pin on a grenade and lobbed it into the office before running for the door.

In her memory she felt the shock of the explosion at her back, pushing her forward, while in front of her the world on the other side of the Veil was turning to dull gray. Damcar gradually came into focus over Daath's shoulder. If she still possessed a mouth she would have laughed at the sight of heaven. A grouping of holes and hovels! If this was not further proof that this world needed to be destroyed, she didn't know what was. It was the type of place where she would expect to find the last burial place of God, with a tombstone which read, "Here lies God, vindictive, difficult to work with, and a miserable son of a bitch when it came to fair play, but what a sense of humor, if you like sarcasm. Good riddance." It was a place that paled in the light of expectation. Then again, the view of the Tower was amazing, and maybe there were other hidden miracles that were not apparent at first glance.

But she didn't have time to go in search of miracles right now. Ignoring Alma and Blake as they walked off, she tried to figure out what she could do without a body. She had hoped that her body would reconstitute on this side of the Veil, but no such luck. What could she do as pure consciousness?

Concentrating, she pulled at Daath's robes. Nothing. It seemed she was unable to physically affect reality in this fashion. Then she looked into Daath's dark eyes and got an idea.

Not sure whether this would work, she entered Daath's ear and worked her way into its brain. It did not fight or resist. Its mind, like its body, seemed in constant flux. As she explored its memories, she realized that its body reacted to the multiple strands of memory it encountered simultaneously. This led to its fluctuating deformities, as its limbs would appear in multiple dimensions and then solidify on one side of the Veil or the other. It was a singular creature, with the ability to perceive multiple dimensions simultaneously. Its mind did not have the built-in genetic code that shut this faculty down in ordinary humans.

Daath had experienced all the revelatory experiences of the millions of souls it had shuttled through the Veil. Her memory was here; he knew she had hitched a ride. As a stowaway, she had not given a token. Then she thought about it: yes, she had, her body had been her token. That was the thing she was most attached to, the thing that she needed to let go of. She would have been barred had she not given this up. She had relied heavily on her body, but at the same time it was only capable of so much. To move on she had to move past it.

Curios about this creature's origins, she dug through its memories trying to go back to its very first memory. Its earliest memories were not of birth, but of its attempt to cross the Veil. Not having a map or knowledge, it became lost within the limbo. Other souls were trapped there, unable to find the other side or get back to the primordial Strands. But this one was an ancient alchemist, a man of power who had searched all his life for transformation and epiphany.

As he encountered other lost and wandering beings in the Veil, he slit their throats, opened their chests, and ingested their hearts. He was a killer, but not like Macaria. He took no pleasure in the act, and

his victims were willing participants. Most had spent millennia in
the gray, unchanging haze of the Veil. As he ate the heart of each one,
their monumental experiences were revealed to him. He stored it in
his brain and slowly grew more powerful. The combined will of all
those memories led him in a subtle way towards the other side of the
Veil, the Nexus and the Tower, the only place where such revelations
could be fully explored.

When he entered Damcar, he knew he was home. The Geburiak
had sacrificed their humanity to the Strands and could not tell him
their own history or how such a place came to be, but they knew of
his purpose: to be Daath, a being with the knowledge to cross the
abyss. His ability to house the revelations of others made him the
only creature they had met that could accomplish such a thing.

He did not question any of this. He had searched his whole life for
purpose and here it was. He could live within sight of the beginning
of the universe and be part of the engine that kept it evolving. He did
what he felt drawn to do, becoming a creature of instinct. He gave up
his capacity to judge experience, and equally enjoyed the moments
of beauty, love, terror, and horror. He simply existed, and did what
he felt compelled to do.

The visitors all pitied him, but he felt no shame, felt no self-pity.
He was more content then anyone he'd ever brought across the Veil.
And in that way, was he not the true master? Had he not unwittingly
uncovered the transforming alchemy and ingested the philosopher's
stone, turning the base metal of his body into spiritual gold?

Macaria took control easily. It was an experience Daath was used
to and one he did not judge or attempt to qualify. Macaria felt dizzy
as she attempted to move Daath's right arm which had a bone and
muscle structure that seemed to flux as she willed it to flex. As she

focused her sight on the arm it's skin warped, each tick of the arm traveled through the memory of multiple Strands. She felt herself losing control. How was she going to do this? Again she focused, and the harder she tried the worse the storm in her mind became. She tried again and again, failing each time.

Christ. What the Fuck. How am I going to do this? And then realization dawned. To pass the Veil she had to give up her body, but there was another token she was even less willing to relinquish, control. Her life had been guided by a force of will, a will to power, to control her mind and her body. To pull the strings of this puppet she needed to let go, to become one with it. Only then would it become hers to use.

Macaria stopped pushing. She allowed the wave of the Strands to wash over her as she relaxed into the chaos. When she clenched her fist and brought it up to her face in victory there was a momentary flash of disorientation but she did not focus on the shifting patterns of flesh and bone. Daath had become Death.

The dagger, the one that had seen Daath through the Veil, still stained with the blood of those transforming hearts, hung from a pocket within its cape. Macaria took it out and examined its sharp, curved blade.

She saw that Blake and Alma were at the far side of Damcar, walking towards the Nexus and the tower. She could ignore them for now. She searched Daath's brain, thumbing through the catalog of his memory. There were fifty Geburiak in Damcar. Daath had never seen a Geburiak attacked or killed so it had no idea how difficult it would be to kill one. Well, Macaria thought, I guess I'll have to do a test run.

She entered one of the Damcar dwellings. The Geburiak sitting on the floor did not move or resist as she put the knife blade against its throat and pulled hard. The skin or substance that made up their bodies offered no resistance to the blade; it was like cutting through warm butter. The head flopped backward, dangling by a thread, and a flash of light spilled from its neck. The light was like a flashbang grenade, burning her retinas. She looked away and when she looked back the entire body had become a soupy pool on the floor of the dwelling. It then began to seep into the sand and disappeared. It was as if it had never been.

This was very similar to what the crabs had done for her, and she couldn't tell whether this meant death here was more permanent or less. Would the Geburiak return now? Had she merely transformed it? Was she in fact their savior, rescuing them from these ancient arcane bodies that had prevented them from achieving revelation? It was impossible to know, but there was only one path now: kill them all and see what happened.

She walked into all the huts and caves and performed the same act with the same results. When she had only five left to go, she began to notice an increase in pressure. Her ears popped. As she turned to look at the Veil, she saw that it had transformed from an undulating sea of mist into a solid mirror—and the mirror was cracking.

Turning to look at the Nexus, she saw another change. The tight web now showed spaces between the Strands, a giant knot loosening, ready to accept entry.

Alma and Blake had turned around and were staring at Daath—at her. She could see that they understood. Death had taken control.

The remaining five Geburiak stood in a line, observing the Nexus and the Tower with vacant black eyes, lining up as if for a firing squad. Macaria walked down the line. With each throat she slit, there was an increase in atmospheric pressure. The mirror cracked deeply, sounding like glacial ice, shifting and rumbling. An earthquake began to shake Damcar as the butte that had been the home of the Geburiak began sinking into a deep fissure. Another slit throat and the mirror exploded. More fissures opened in the ground, and the pressure became painful.

Macaria instantly understood what was happening. By destroying the Geburiak she was killing the holy instant. She was erasing the timelessness of this place and it was collapsing in on itself.

She moved down the line.

As she reached the last of the Geburiak, she paused for a moment. She knew she couldn't kill this one and survive. Would the collapse of Damcar mean the death of the Tower, of the Strands? Would she have accomplished her goal? Or was this all she could do this time around?

She looked at the last Geburiak and had an idea. She held the knife against its throat and began to push it towards the Nexus. If she waited until they were close to the Nexus and then slit its throat, she could jump into the rainbow threads and hope that she would be pulled through the Nexus and into the Tower. She wanted to experience the end to make sure it was all destroyed and if she were to die in Damcar the Tower and the Strands may live on. She was determined to make sure that didn't happen. She wanted to see it all dead. To see the light to go out of the Strands as they became gray twisted withering snakes. To watch as the Tower crumbled to the ground, its dark occupant screaming as it fell from its perch on the balcony becoming one with the rubble that rained upon the upturned slack stupid faces of Blake and Alma as they were crushed. Only then could she die. Only then would it be done.

She pushed again and was caught unawares as the Geburiak drew its throat across the knife's blade. There was a final blinding flash.

She didn't know whether this would be true death or just the death of this form. Was this just another door? As the collapse began, gravity stretching and compressing her, she knew that she had only completed one part of her assault. The Tower would have to wait for another lifetime. The Geburiak, by taking its own life, had doomed her first attempt to failure. But she would try again. In her last conscious moment, she thought, In my next life I will be back and finish this.

CHaPTer 17

When the Veil shattered, Blake knew that their only hope was to enter the Nexus. Damcar was being crushed like a star collapsing into a black hole. He could feel the increase in gravity, the pull toward dark inevitability. Whatever magic the Geburiak possessed had kept Damcar alive, and with the last of them dead, the holy instant was being obliterated from existence.

"We have to go!" Alma yelled. "The Tower is our only chance now."

She pulled at Blake's hand. He stood still, staring at Daath wondering why it would destroy its home. Then his perception changed and he understood that Daath was now only a costume of flesh for Macaria, the goddess of death. She had defied all barriers, crossed the Veil, possessed Daath and killed the Geburiak, but still her ultimate objective eluded her. Blake could feel the gathering energy, the hair on his arms standing up, the Strands preparing to defend against annihilation.

He saw the raging storm of colors flash through the last Geburi-ak's eyes as it destroyed itself on her blade. Blake shielded his eyes from the flash of light that shot from its neck. That beam of light was a beacon of hope for the Strands. The Goddess raised Daath's three arms in defiance of her defeat and screamed. The Veil shattered, and Blake saw Daath reduced to tatters by the rain of shards. It was the last thing he saw of Damcar as the percussive force lifted and pushed them forward into the Nexus.

The ethereal tentacles of the Strands wrapped around him. Before he was completely engulfed, he heard something like a thunderclap and then the softest of sighs as the holy instant was crushed and removed from existence—and Macaria with it.

Entering the Nexus was like entering a turbulent storm of emotions, thoughts, and images. The two of them were tossed into the midst of millions of lives, choices, and dreams. They flashed by and through, catching a moment in time of each raw emotion. The thoughts, the images, the sounds were a kaleidoscope of sensation that threatened to pitch both of them into insanity. Unlike Daath, they were not made for this; their minds would shatter like the Veil. But as Damcar imploded behind them, a shock wave ripped through the Nexus and the various Strands separated, and they found respite in the empty spaces between.

Alma was holding Blake's hand in a death grip. To become separated was to be lost indefinitely. Together they stood a chance. While one became entrapped in a strand, the other struggled forward in the empty space created by the percussive force of Damcar's destruction. Perpetual forward motion was the key as they pressed forward one exhausting step at a time, each taking a turn to drag the other forward. To stop was to become enraptured and lost in the story of the Strands. They were of one mind, one purpose: make it to the Tower.

In the reality or dimension of the Tower, a field of roses surrounded its base. In those moments when Blake was able to worm his way through the gaps in the Strands, he saw the most beatific vision of the black Tower erupting from this crimson field, a sultry wind blowing across the roses, wafting their aroma into his face. The petals screamed red and the onyx tower absorbed their bloody reflection, glowing red at its base. It was a surreal vision one that could inspire poetic madness.

He pulled Alma with him, holding her hand tightly, his vision of the Tower overwhelmed by the Strands. They would crash over him like a wave, slamming him with pain, joy, loss, kisses, beatific vistas, awesome dreams, bloody nightmares. His vision would partially clear and he'd see the roses through a haze, and then the undertow would grab at him, some painful emotion slowing his feet. Sometimes he pushed forward and dragged Alma with him; sometimes she dragged him. He wondered whether he was hurting her, but there was nothing he could do about it now. He hoped they would make it to the Tower with at least some of their sanity intact.

After what seemed like hours, they were close. He'd seen the visions of thousands of souls, the nightmares of thousands more. He'd felt their pain; he'd seen their joy. It was a constant balancing act between love, hate, pain and passion with no winners or losers.

As they struggled beneath the shadow of the Tower's portal, the Strands tightened. There were no more gaps. The ethereal fingers wormed into his brain, thousands of images pushing into his mind; there was no black or white, no 1 or 0, there was only the All, and it was killing him, driving him mad.

Somewhere, in some other world, he could feel a tug on his arm, insistent, growing in intensity. The million movie screen images flashed once, twice—

And there was darkness as his head cleared the Nexus. Above him, looking down, was Alma, her eyes wild but sane. She'd dragged him out of the Strands to a landing at the bottom of a dark circular staircase.

"Blake, can you hear me?"

He nodded but couldn't speak.

She sat down next to him. He couldn't tell whether she was laughing or crying. Maybe a combination of both.

He propped himself up on his elbows and looked at the writhing Strands. They entered a hole in the center of the tower and then disappeared upward. The staircase wound around this luminous central pillar.

He glanced over his shoulder at Alma, who sat with her head in her hands. "Are you all right?"

"Fuck, Blake, I don't know anymore." She forced a smile but it didn't reach her eyes, which were filled with concern and confusion. "Spent all my life wondering what the point was. Wondering if I could find the thing that explained everything. When I found music I thought that was it—well, most of the time I thought that was it, but every once in a while I'd feel this darkness, this incompleteness, like there was just something missing. Like there was one more thing to find. Is that what you feel?"

Blake nodded. "Except I feel it most of the time."

Her expression changed to one of pity. "That's too bad."

There was nothing else either of them could say, nothing to discuss or decide. There was no way to go back. They could only go forward and hope for the best.

CHaPTer 18

Blake felt that there was a time when he could have sat there hold-ing Alma's hand and stared at the splendor of the Nexus forever. He watched as the strands wove their way into the base of the Tower and then ascended up to wherever they ended—Heaven? As amazing and miraculous as this was, experience had taken away his awe at the rich colors and flashy opalescence. Now he knew there was pain and darkness woven into the fabric of epiphany. Ecstatic vision wasn't for the faint; it was for those willing to crawl through the darkness hoping to discover a diamond. More often than not you would only find mud and rock. You might grasp something, full of hope, and wash the muck away, only to realize that all you had was a piece of fossilized shit. Sitting here now, he had to wonder whether what was at the top of this Tower was it the diamond he sought or just a turd—or nothing at all.

And of course there was still the possibility that all of this was just in his head, a complex nightmare—a deeper, darker psychosis.

"Shall we?" he asked Alma, not wanting to waste any more time in contemplation.

"Sooner begun, sooner done," Alma quipped.

Hand in hand, they wove their way up the Tower. The interior was constructed of that same smoky dark glass. The flames of the Strands could be seen darkly through the central tube as they walked up the steps. On occasion there was a landing with an opening into the tunnel of the Strands. Blake got the idea that they were maintenance panels, as if the engineer of this madness would walk up and down the Tower checking on the Strands and making measurements and adjustments as necessary. Maybe that was one of the tasks of the dark figure that watched from the balcony.

They had been walking upward for a time when they came upon one of these openings. There was beautiful music issuing from it: a voice that fluctuated between demon and angel, a symphony of instruments. Anywhere else, he had no doubt, it would sound like an atonal mess, but here the ear was more open, there was some form of magic at work. It was as if every tone, every instrument, everything that made noise was gathered here into this singular refrain, an ode to music itself, capturing its very essence.

Alma approached it. She had a smile on her face, her eyes sparkling. She had found her diamond.

"I can't go any farther."

"What? You can't go back. The only way—"

"I return here." She turned to look at him. "Alex was wrong, Blake. I'm not a savior soul type. I'm not one of those people who has to know it all. Those burning questions give me purpose. It's the search for answers that gives my life meaning, not finding them."

Blake didn't know what to say. He heard her words but could not find meaning in them. He could not comprehend not wanting to go on, not wanting that final answer, even if that answer was meaningless. His search for answers had stopped being a passion long ago. Now he was fully willing to admit that it was pure addiction. He could stop for nothing at this point. Whatever he was would not allow him to do so.

"I think Alex had it right," he finally said.

She hugged him and stared into his eyes. He didn't know what he'd do without her, but he knew she couldn't go on and he couldn't go back. For now, at least, their journeys took separate Strands.

She did not say goodbye. She simply turned and stepped into the Strands. There was a flash of light, an elevation in the volume of the music as Alma added her momentous note, and then she was gone and Blake stood alone.

CHAPTER 19

Alma Vida stepped into the Strands and for a moment there was nothing but warm white light, followed by that one perfect eternal note that told the story of the universe, echoing in her ears. Alma blinked. The note stopped, and she was standing at the back of the stage of the Soul Fly looking out past the stacked guitar amplifiers at a hushed crowd. The stage was wrapped in silence. Derick the drummer of Dark-Revelations was staring at her, twirling a drum stick between his fingers in nervous anticipation, waiting.

She had expected some sort of rebirth, or perhaps eternal communion with the essence of music. How could she be brought back to her own self? Had her body been standing here like an empty shell, just waiting for her to return? Since her departure had and alternate version of herself continued to show up at the Soul Fly to perform with Dark-Revelations? Had this reality simply stalled waiting for the actors on the stage to be refilled with consciousness? How long had she been standing here? Had she ever left? Had it all been a dream lived out in her mind as she sat backstage waiting for their set to begin? So many questions coursed through her mind as she struggled to understand what had happened. What was real? What was fantasy? Did it make any difference?

Magix was standing to the right of her at the edge of the stage. He was stroking his chin looking both contemplative and concerned as he examined her. He tilted his head towards the front of the stage and when she didn't take any action he made a get-out-there-what-are-you-waiting-for gesture with his hands.

She felt a surge of emotions, confusion, passion, pain, hate, love as her awareness became reincarnated in the dimension of her birth. It was a swell that she needed to purge. She felt the familiar weight of the microphone in her right hand and brought it to her lips and let out a feral, primordial scream. The scream echoed through the Soul Fly as she stepped past the amplifiers and took center stage. The crowd erupted in response, stage lights focused white beams upon her, a star blazing in the black of space. As she gazed outward she understood her purpose. Before, she had talent, she had stories to tell, and she had love, but now she had knowledge as well. She knew of the Strands and had the ability to recreate that knowledge with her music.

As the echo of her birth scream was dying, her eyes went to a figure standing in the back by the bar. Alex. She could see from his shocked expression how rare this event was. She didn't know how long she'd been gone or how many times he'd come back hoping to find her here, but she could see from his haggard expression that he'd almost given up. That expression slowly shifted to happiness and then to hope. At that moment she knew it had all been real. She would never understand the whole thing, pieces were missing, logic and time gaps became gaping holes in the picture of her reality but none of that mattered now, for being able to explain it didn't change it.

Her purpose was now linked with his. They would share the truth of the Strands with everyone. And they would expose the evil cruelties of the Strand Corporation as they taught the world how to trade in their belief in lies and false prophets for truth and salvation.

The stage lights went dead and she was enveloped in darkness. The crowd fell silent once again. She felt a power in her she hadn't known before and immediately identified it: she had become a Conductor.

She whispered into the microphone, "Let us begin."

She placed the microphone into its clip on the stand and formed a power cord on the fret board of her guitar and began to circle her arm in a typical Townshend windmill motion, colors leaping and dancing from her fingertips. She sang of a journey that began when people opened their eyes to the possibility of life, of going beyond present knowledge to a deeper place, exploring a deeper dark. The crowd was hypnotized.

She sang of the dark dagger that pierced them, the rapturous pain it brought, and the truth it released. She could see they felt it: the needle point just above the bridge of the nose, the moment of possibility. Now, she told them, the daggers tip would be slowly removed and the revelatory vacuum created.

Alma opened a dimension in this void and pushed the expanded dimension forward. Awestruck eyes stared back; mouths gaped. This was not a trinket or a trick; this was true epiphany.

She saw the light in their eyes, the promise of miracle. With one more swing of her arm she expanded the alternate dimension, releasing the full experience of it to the crowd. None would ever be the same again. Nor would she.

CHapTer 20

It seemed hours before Blake reached what he assumed was the top of the Tower. The Strand conduit burned below his feet, the floor glowing with its rainbow colors, disappearing to his left below a doorway of white light. The light was so bright he knew it would blind him if he did not look away. He shifted his gaze to his right, where he saw the balcony and the dark figure.

Slowly the figure turned from its perch and looked at him. Its eyes were dark. As it moved, Blake realized it was not wearing a tattered cape; it seemed entirely made of tendrils of shadow. Its form floated towards him recreated each instant as tendrils of night stitched together to create the appearance of solidity. As it got closer, Blake could see that it had no human features; it just mimicked the form of a person. No eyes or mouth, just the basic shape. At times the form would flash like a flame, colors flickering within and then disappearing. It was a projection of the Strands, taking on a form for a purpose he did not understand. But like Daath, it was meant to help him. What lesson it had in store, he could only guess at.

It did not touch him but engulfed him, wrapping him in a blanket of night. His life flashed before him in a moment: all his experiences, his hopes, his dreams, his failures, relationships, a life of myriad choices. He saw the lives of all the people he had touched or influenced, directly through actual contact or indirectly through his writing and poetry. From there the web spread outward, all the lives of those people, their choices, their dreams, the people they had helped or harmed, and out again. Each time the sphere grew until it was all-encompassing. As he moved outward, he went forwards and backwards in time until there seemed no continuity. There was pain, pleasure, wars, peace, despair, separation. It was the gamut of all human emotion. He experienced it all in an instant and when it was done it started all over again.

There were periods of unity; there were individuals who would see the truth, their light shining like supernovae through the architecture of the strands. Alma was just such a supernova, an explosion of spiritual energy, touching everything, bringing the whole closer. And more than just understanding, she recreated the holy instant, that moment out of time, where one not only understood the concept of All but truly felt it. Souls such as these were the saviors with the courage to find the diamond and be elevated above the abyss, returning to show that diamond to the rest of the world.

But not him. Alex was wrong. He'd been off by an inch. Blake was not the savior but the saved.

Whatever there was that could be learned in a million million lifetimes, he experienced. Finally, this Soul Tool had nothing more to teach and therefore he had no reason to return. Alex had that correct, at least. There was a limit to human experience.

As the dark tendrils wove through Blake's mind, he became the embodiment of the Strands. He became the Tower in microcosm. The Strands allowed one to experience the entire human journey and then take the next step beyond.

The gift given, the dark figure retreated from his mind, evaporating and then reforming as it returned to its post at the balcony, waiting for the next traveler.

To Blake's left was another doorway of light that led to his answers. Blake approached and stopped, feeling scared, knowing he would go on but wanting to take a moment to bask in the light of knowledge.

He had arrived. Beyond this there would be no more. The him on the other side of the light would no longer exist. The world as he understood it would no longer exist.

He did not turn as he took this last step. There was nothing to see behind him. All humankind traveled with and through him. For a moment he felt the overwhelming peace of a long journey finally ending. His whole body sighed and laughed. It was time to remember the one thing he had forgotten: who and what he truly was.

He stepped into the light.

The End

THank you

Dear reader, word of mouth is crucial as an indie writer. If you enjoyed the book, please consider leaving a review. This can be a sentence or as long as you wish, every little bit helps and is appreciated.

For news about Dark Revelations Media, our latest releases, and special promotional offers, join our newsletter at www.darkrevme dia.com. Your email address will never be shared, and you can unsubscribe at any time.

Masks of God – The Tin Man

A childhood prank turns violent, giving Austin his first glimpse of true evil. Traumatized, branded a coward, this Tin Man goes in search of his heart, embarking on a mysterious journey that brings him in contact with shamans, monks, occultists, and otherworldly beings that tell of a Mask that can unlock hidden powers of those who wear it. Will the Mask reveal the secret Tin has been searching for? Or will his obsession with it lead only to insanity? Only the Mask can tell.

Get you FREE ebook copy at: https://darkrevmedia.com/mogt-inman

ALSO BY Brian White

<u>Horn & Dagger</u>

<u>The Invincible – A Veils of the Witch Story</u>

<u>In the Shadow of the Witch – Veils of the Witch Book 1</u>

<u>Rise of the Witch – Veils of the Witch Book 2</u>

<u>Masks of God – The Tin Man</u>

ABOUT THE AUTHOR

Brian White is the author of The Strands, Horn and Dagger, In the Shadow of the Witch Veils of the Witch Book 1, Rise of the Witch Veils of the Witch Book 2 and Masks of God -The Tin Man. He lives in New Jersey with his wife and two daughters. Brian holds a bachelor's degree in Psychology from FDU. His interest in psychology let to his studies of philosophy, mythology and mysticism, all subjects that have had a strong influence on his writing. He explores these subjects in depth on the Dark Thoughts page of the www.darkrevmedia.com site. In addition, music has been an important part of his life. In particular, his writing has been influenced by heavy metal music with its dark, frenetic energy, and thought-provoking themes and lyrics. On the Dark Tunes page of the site, Brian explores the role that specific bands, albums, and songs have played in his creative, storytelling process. When not writing Brian enjoys reading, playing guitar and mountain biking.

Learn more about the author at: www.darkrevmedia.com Or contact him directly at: brianwhite@darkrevmedia.com

www.ingramcontent.com/pod-product-compliance
Lightning Source LLC
Chambersburg PA
CBHW022122170626
46808CB00002B/811